Ella Dietz

The Triumph of Life

Mystical Poem

Ella Dietz

The Triumph of Life
Mystical Poem

ISBN/EAN: 9783337371890

Printed in Europe, USA, Canada, Australia, Japan

Cover: Foto ©Andreas Hilbeck / pixelio.de

More available books at **www.hansebooks.com**

THE TRIUMPH OF LIFE.

Mystical Poem.

BY

ELLA DIETZ,

AUTHOR OF—"THE TRIUMPH OF LOVE"; "THE TRIUMPH OF TIME."

LONDON:
E. W. ALLEN, 4, AVE MARIA LANE.
MDCCCLXXXV.

שִׁירֵי לְיִשְׂרָאֵל

לְבָבִי לַיהֹוָה

" The day is short and the work is great but the labourers are idle, though the reward be great and the Master of the work presses. It is not incumbent upon thee to complete the work; but thou must not therefore cease from it."—THE TALMUD.

" With stammering lips and another tongue will he speak to this people."—ISAIAH xxviii. 11.

Part I.

THE CROSS.

"The Altar is the Cross. The souls under the Altar are the souls under the Cross or these that are crucified with Jesus; these having passed the mystic death in the fourth central number where light is generated from the Cross, begin to arise in the next holy number, till at length they attain the Sabbath of their rest in the seventh, in which the Divine Spirit is fully manifested and the soul fully perfected."

" The process of mystical death consists in a sevenfold purification and refining according to the number and order of the seals."

" The new generation of the soul is a passing out of darkness into light through the power of the Lamb raising up himself therein and redeeming it from the wrathful source of nature in its dark and fiery principles."

" This internal resurrection and redemption brings the spirit of the soul through all the seals of nature, into the very substantiality of Christ's universal body, the principle and centre of light eternal, where Wisdom reigns in the wonders of God."

" The regenerated spirit draws after it the soul, and that also draws the body without which it cannot be perfected, and so the soul is clothed upon with the heavenly body of the inward Christ."

"This inward Christ, or CHRIST FORMED WITHIN, is the *new creature* and is one with Jesus Christ, sitting in the heavenly places, at the right hand of the Father, being spirit of His spirit and flesh of His flesh."

" Thus the saints are one body in Him and He is this body in God : they enter into His humanity and He becomes man in them.

" By this new generation or New Birth of spirit, soul and body is the *new* man perfected in Christ, and reigns with Christ in the new garment of his body completely put on by virtue of the *seventh seal* broken up in the Lamb's nature."

" The process of the mystic resurrection, and the *first resurrection* (which follows immediately hereupon) and the manifestation of it is to be looked for under the mystery of the *seven thunders.*"

THE CROSS.

I.

Ah! well-a-day, thou didst not miss me long;

Has the last echo died of that low song

I sang for thee erewhile? Hast thou no fear

Of a day that must come soon when on the bier

I shall lie cold, my heart as calm as thine?

Then wilt thou weep? Behold! I shall be strong

Then may'st thou sigh, yet wake no sigh of mine,

On my white cheek there then will shine no tear

Unless from thy sad eyes some tear-drops fall;

Weep on, sob on, it will not me appal;

Soon shall the death-smile on my face appear,

And then thy grief can vex me not at all.

II.

Ah ! well-a-day, the sun shines bright and clear,
 But then I shall not know, I shall not care ;
Wilt thou bring flowers, pale flowers, and lay them near
 My face, which death shall make so white and fair ?
A pale, pale bride that will not speak nor stir ?
Though roses red and white be strewn for her ;
 She seems to sleep, and sleeping dream of peace,
 Then wake her not lest her sweet dream should cease ;
Let the frail flowers in silence minister.

III.

Ah ! well-a-day, she with the flowers must hide ;
 Far out of sight, among dark hidden things
Where rootlets creep and grow, she must abide
 Till from her fading form new vigor springs.
So green the grass above the crumbling mould ;
A few white lilies in the pale hands fold,
 The hands that shall again the lilies bring.

IV.

Ah! well-a-day, so soon to say farewell
  To the sad lips that answer not again ;
Does she not hear ? Alas! she cannot tell,
  She will not speak to us of joy or pain,
She will not speak, she will not breathe or sigh ;
We call in vain, the dead make no reply ;
  They feel no sun, they feel no falling rain.
We stand and weep by them a little while,
  Then in the cold dark earth we lay away
The face that cannot weep but only smile,
  Waiting the coming of perpetual day.

V.

Ah ! well-a-day, when Death doth walk so near,

    Why should we grieve so much ? why should we
        chide ?

Laid in the grave, equals we shall appear—

    The strong and weak alike in earth must hide—

When from thy heart a slender lily grows,

Then from my breast shall spring a fadeless rose,

    And sweetly they will bloom there side by side,

Shedding their fragrance on the summer air ;

Perchance some child will watch them growing there,

    While we, unconsciously, in sleep repose.

VI.

Ah ! well-a-day, the night is now far spent,
   The rays of the new morning swift advance,
And we must fold the curtains of our tent
   To travel onward armed with spear and lance ;
We know not when our journey shall be done,
But we must travel onward, every one—
   The pageant moves like slow majestic dance.

VII.

Ah ! well-a-day, one common fate for all—
   Smiles, tears and joys, and then a bier and shroud ;
Whatever chance, this surely shall befall,
   We must pass out of sight beyond the cloud.
Then since our destiny doth make us one,
Let us forgive the ills that each hath done ;
   Before the face of unrelenting Death
   Let us use well our little grant of breath,
Till each shall go where none can him recall.

VIII.

Ah ! well-a-day, our life doth pass so soon—

The morning past, comes on the sultry noon.

And then the shades of evening settle down.

Ah ! chide me not, I cannot bear thy frown,

Knowing the day of parting must soon come :

The " passing bell " shall toll one spirit home,

And then the peace of death our love shall crown.

Death that wipes out all stains and scars, shall make

The soul at peace, e'en though the torn heart ache ;

There is a majesty in that last sleep

That bids us honour it, e'en while we weep

Above the face that never more shall wake,

Until the everlasting morning break.

IX.

Ah ! well-a-day, we all must enter in

    The self-same door ; the living do but wait

To follow thee ; thy life doth now begin ;

    O, thou who now hast passed within the gate,

The quick stand sobbing round the helpless clay

That must so soon in earth be laid away,

    Yet they themselves do wait to meet that fate,

Whil'st thou perchance art tasting perfect day,

    With angels that thy coming celebrate,

Rejoiced to bear thee from the realm of sin.

X.

Ah ! well-a-day, we do but battle here,

 Waging long war against satanic power,

And every inch we gain doth cost us dear,

 While life keeps ebbing from us hour by hour.

Oh ! when at last upon the ground I'm laid,

Count not the wounds that sin in me hath made,

 But only look to find the Holy Cross—

 Christ gave it me, I shall not suffer loss,

Nor shall the hour of death make me afraid,

 If I may hold that fast—his precious dower.

XI.

Ah ! well-a-day, that Cross was made for me—
  Symbol so strong, its weight I scarce can bear
And it was carved from out the very tree
  Whereon my Lord was nailed ; yet do I dare
To place it on my lips and on my breast ;
O Saviour in thy Cross can I find rest ?
  Yea, rest, eternal Lord for thou art there ;
That Cross was made and carved by mine own sin,
And yet I find my Saviour's face therein ;
  From out my blackened darkness shines His face,
  And risen glory lightens death's own place.

XII.

O gladsome day! the resurrection morn ;

From Mother Death, O Christ! thou art firstborn—

Firstborn of Mary, blessed fruit of womb—

Firstborn of Mara, bursting from the tomb.

Hast thou not come to call my spirit forth,

From shades of night to give me risen birth ?

Though I be dead, by sin's destruction slain,

Breathe on me, Lord, and I shall live again ;

Say but " arise," and, Saviour, in thy might,

I shall go forth clothed with the Son's own light.

XIII.

O glorious day ! when risen flesh shall be

Re-moulded in thine image like to thee ;

When sons of God thy glory manifest,

When eyes can see and read the vision blest

Of Thee, O Lord, in likeness as thou art,

I shall be satisfied with every part

When I awake perfected by thine eye

Which heart and reins doth search, and searching try,

I shall be satisfied ; do thou create

The creature new in me—new Adam's mate.

I kiss the Cross whereon my Saviour died ;

I kiss the Cross where God was justified ;

Though man's most hideous act hath nailed him there,

His love hath made that place of darkness fair,

His love hath made Golgotha's gloom to shine,

The barren tomb brings forth the man Divine.

SUB SILENTIO.

I.

Good-bye, my silent one,

Thy silence speaks for thee

More than earth's loudest tone,

More than the groaning sea;

Thy stilly silence reaches from afar,

Piercing my soul like beams from northern star.

Good-bye to lips grown still,

Good-bye to saddened eyes,

Good-bye to the stern will

Stifling the deep heart-cries;

Thy silence teaches me the better part,

Thy silence reaches me where'er thou art.

When in the pale midnight
   The moon shines calm and cold,
When with her mantle white,
   Winter the earth doth fold;
Viewing the frozen scene I feel thee near -
Visions of spring upon the hills appear.

   Fetter thy spirit free,
      Clasp it in chains,
   Yet would it speak to me
      Through frost and rains,
Through fire and flood, through seas, through
   desert sand,
Thy spirit seeks my heart—its native land.

   Nowhere beneath the skies
      Can it repose,
Save sunk within mine eyes,
      Under the rose—
A sacred flower that guards where true love sleeps,
And ever vigil for the faithful keeps.

'Biding our time, we wait,

 Sundered, yet one,

Futures shall compensate,

 God's Will be done ;

The path of duty we are strong to tread,

There shall we find from Him our daily bread.

Father, watch over us,

 Guard us from sin,

Keep us and cover us,

 Close us within ;

Upon the floods thy doves can find no rest,

Open the ark and hide us in thy breast.

THE CHERUBIM.

EZEKIEL I. X.

Out of the whirlwind from the north,
   Out of the amber fire,
O Cherubim, shine forth, shine forth,
   Moving with one desire.

Under the deep blue sapphire stone,
   Under the crystal sea,
Under the Man upon the Throne
   Shine forth with will set free.

Eight wings are lifted up on high,
   Kissing in close embrace;
Eight wings do cover as they fly—
   Cherub with fourfold face.

Angel and man and beast and bird,
    With powers of instant flight,
They moved, the noise of wings I heard,
    And saw the flash of light.

Under the firmament they stood,
    Their wings were folded down ;
On each side two, on each side two ;
    Above, a fiery crown.

They moved, they went, I heard the sound
    Of many waters rush ;
The Voice whose richest tones abound
    Where living fountains gush.

The voice, as of a multitude ;
    The noise as of a host ;
They went as by one power imbued,
    Moved by the Holy Ghost.

The cloud of glory round them shone,
  Encircled by the bow ;
The Voice spake now, as from the Throne.
  The Spirit made them go.

The Spirit went, the creature went,
  The fourfold power o'ercame,
Lifting from earth in high ascent,
  Receivers of the Name.

O fourfold power ! O fourfold life !
  Long, long have ye withstood
The balance that could heal your strife,
  The unity of good.

O fourfold life ! O fourfold power !
  Under the firmament
The whirlwind and the fiery hour
  Know when your spirits blent.

Under the shining sapphire stone,

Under the crystal sea,

Under the Man upon the Throne,

Shine forth with will set free.

PURIFICATION.

I do not ask to stand within thy sight,
  O my belovèd, as I once have stood,
  Holding thy love—crown of my womanhood,
And clothed with woven wonders of delight;
I would not wield my sceptre, if I might,
  Commanding thee to see only my good;
  Nor feed thee now with that supernal food
Grown where celestial day absorbs the night;
Nay, now my soul must dwell in valleys low
  Till purging fires do cleanse away its stains,
While ceaseless tears, that like sad rivers flow,
  Bring penitence and its strong healing pains;
My darkest sin I there shall learn to know,
  And from what pit my soul its heaven regains.

PALM SUNDAY.

I.

Thy spirit keeps its tryst with mine,
Thy heart doth call me home,
Thy love doth comfort me like wine,
Oh ! gladly will I come ;
My soul like the swift hind doth flee,
Climbing its heights to dwell with thee.

Thine eyes do glow with heavenly light
Fairer than moon or star,
Thy goodly countenance made bright
With beauty nought can mar,
The holy rapture of thy face
Portrays thy soul's immortal grace.

My head is laid upon thy breast,
  And woes of parting fade ;
With peace of God and holy rest,
  Our anguish is repaid;
Our struggling hearts we did uplift
To Him, and now He gives His gift.

We find our home builded on high ;
  Cleansed by the fires of love,
We reach the City in the sky—
  Jerusalem above—
Our Mother, whose illumined law
Has purged away each stain and flaw.

We pass within the pearly gates,
  We walk the golden streets ;
The world and its contrary fates
  And sorrows now retreats ;
Its strife and discord fade away
In visions of eternal day.

Together, 'neath the living Tree,
  We pluck the sacred fruit ;
Eternal now our life shall be,
  Grown from one holy root ;
In Him we move and breathe and live,
To Him our aspirations give.

With one desire we move to Him—
  The Author of our joy—
Our brightness now shall never dim,
  Our gold know no alloy,
Nor death nor hell can work us harm
Beneath the everlasting arm.

He died for us, in Him we die ;
  He lives and is our life ;
He has ascended up on high—
  The conqueror of all strife ;
The everlasting Prince of Peace,
Whose coming makes all wars to cease.

Two holy hearts begin His reign,
>Two hearts, where love doth dwell,
Exalted beyond earthly pain,
>Redeemed from death and hell;
In stainless hearts He finds His home,—
Immanuel! Thy kingdom come!

PALM SUNDAY.

II.

There's not a cloud in the sky,
>Mild is the balmy air;
Thy spirit draweth nigh,
>Borne on the wings of prayer;
The sky above, like a sapphire stone
Shines blue, deep blue, as the shining Throne;
>And the day is calm and still,
>Calm as my heart and will.

The Church's door I enter

And gaze at the Church's centre—

　The Altar, pure and white,

　Where gleams the warm sunlight

Filtered through crimson and purple panes,—

The steps are bright with its rainbow stains;

And behind the great palm branches green

Spread, and the Cross of Calvary screen—

　The Cross now hidden there,

　That soon will shine so bare.

I kneel, and the first far-distant notes

Of the choir are heard, and the music floats

　Adown the aisles, and Paradise

　Seems near, so near; O heart, arise!

Thy Lord and Saviour draweth nigh,

　Fling down thy palms before His feet;

Lo! the desire of every eye

  Doth come; rise, make His pathway sweet,

With garments the rough way cover,

Spread the fig trees' branches over,

    And the willows of the brook;

      Judah's prevailing Lion

      Is coming unto Zion,

    Meekly upon the ass,

    Down the steep mountain pass,

      And gentle is His look;

    Hosanna! shout Hosanna!

      And down the branches fling,

    Hosanna to the Highest!

      Oh welcome, David's King!

We kneel together there,

  Thy spirit close to mine,

And from my heart escapes a prayer—

    " Union in the Divine ";

May God's own body heal us twain,

And make us one in Him again ;

  O mystic bread and wine

  That art to us the sign

Of perfect union in the Lord ;

The Bride by her dear Spouse adored,

    Now cleansed by His pure blood,

    Strengthened by that sweet food,

Feels, with ecstatic thrill,

His Will absorb her will,

    Feels the Incarnate Word

Subdue her veins and holy zeal,

Pants for the hour that shall reveal

    The Bridegroom and the Bride.

" I shall be satisfied

When I awake "—O thought too deep

For human words ; in silence keep

And treasure in thine heart

The Word now given,

Choosing the " better part,"

Give earth for heaven.

Lord, in Thy path I fling

Palms, and Hosannas sing ;

Rule now, O Israel's King.

·

A DREAM.

" The poor shall not alway be forgotten ; the patient abiding
of the meek shall not perish forever."

"Arise, O Lord God, and lift up thine hand : forget not the
poor."

Did I dream—that long ago

Thou and I were one ?

That in an evil hour,

Under satanic power,

An evil deed was done ?

Did I dream or do I know ?

Time passes slow,

Yet many years are gone ;

I was so young,

And one with serpent tongue

And serpent ways

Took all my life's young days,

Did me this wrong :

O heart, be strong !

Death will not tarry long.

Yea, was my young life slain ?

Yea, was I taken

Ere love could awaken ?

Bound with a chain ;

O, cruel pain !

Seized as a lamb might be

By eager foe ;

Death sets its victim free :

But death, ah, woe !

Came not to me,

And slow, so slow

The weary years went by as still they go.

And did I dream ? Oh ! why

With sorrow saddened

Did mine eye meet thine eye ?

Why was all gladdened ?

The rose blooms but to die.

My chain I ever wear,

My sorrow I must bear ;

Flesh of his flesh and spirit of thy spirit,

What can my soul inherit ?

What can I call from out the empty air ?

Ah ! what in life or death can my soul merit ?

What but dumb woe, what but a dumb despair ?

Ah, no ! God makes us not for woe,

He will not leave me so.

I am not vanquished quite

By mortal pain ;

I cleave unto the right,

Though I be slain ;

I'll live within God's sight,

And bear my chain.

Living within God's sight,

I shall be free ;

Lord, make my dark way light,

Unveil to me

Thy Will, I yearn with passion for the right,

Make blind eyes see.

Shall I live here but for a little space,

   And then in other realms and spheres awake ?

There shall I meet my loved one, face to face ?

   My thirst be quenched that nought on earth can slake?

      Captivity long borne,

      The resurrection morn

A thousand thousand chains shall snap and break ;

      The captives shall go free

      In righteous liberty

When God the heavens and the earth shall shake.

Part II.

THE RESURRECTION.

"O my Soul! O my Love! Turn I beseech thee and go forth from Vanity, or else thou losest my love and the noble Pearl.

"And thus it comes to pass that the Tree of Pearl in the Garden of Christ is often spoiled : concerning which the scripture maketh a hard knot on conclusion, *viz. : 'That those who have once tasted the sweetness of the world to come, and fall away from it again, shall hardly see the Kingdom of God.'* And though it cannot be denied but that the gates of Grace still stand always open, yet the false and dazzling light of the outward reason of the soul so deceiveth and hindereth such men, that they suppose they have the Pearl, while they yet live in the Vanity of this world and dance with the Devil after his pipe."

"O noble Love give me thy sweet Pearl; put it I pray thee unto me."

"God the Father who gave His dear Heart unto the Humanity to help mankind, doth now thirst after the Humanity."

JACOB BEHMEN.

EASTER MONDAY.

Fair are the lilies far away

That bloom in the Holy Land ;

There shimmering fields of flowers display

The cunning workman's hand.

Bright are the varied rainbow hues

As lustre of metals, the faint steel blues

Quiver in sunlight, like gauzy wings

Of myriad insects ; the light breeze sings

A low love-song as it passes by,

Waving the flowers with its melody.

Fair are the fields where the lilies grow

Tall and white in the golden sun ;

A fountain of gardens is there I know ;

Oh ! to that land could my swift feet run.

Then would a thousand gardens bloom—

Roses and lilies, whose sweet perfume

  Would fill the air with its fragrant breath,

  Till we drank life in and defied grim **Death** :

Blessings of corn and oil and wine,

Flow in the land of the Man Divine.

There would I fain my vineyard keep,

  The tender grapes give a goodly smell :

There would I pasture my Father's sheep,

  Draw the water from Jacob's well.

O hills and vales of my heart's lost home,

When shall thine exile cease to roam ?

  Land of my Fathers ! dear land most fair,

  Laden with spice is thy balmy air ;

When shall mine eyes thy green pastures see,

Drinking the joy of thy liberty ?

Yea pasture thy sheep on our Father's hills

Brother, my brother from days of old ;

The blood is stirred and the new life thrills

With rapture unspoken, with bliss untold.

Figs and pomegranates my garden yields ;

And wells of water in cool green fields,

Are places of rest, and the stranger's way

Is gladdened ; O brother make no delay,

Let us journey thither, yea Zion's song

Shall lead us onward and make us strong.

SONG.

Be thy heart with valour filled

    Brother mine, O brother !

Be thy heart with valour stilled,

    Love divine, O brother !

By thy sword and glittering spear

By thine eye with courage clear,

Chase the foemen pale with fear,

    Brother mine, O brother !

Though their armies be arrayed,

    Brother mine, O brother !

With pick and spear and blade,

    Brother mine, O brother !

Yet shalt thou o'ercome a host,

And drive them from their post,

By power of Holy Ghost,

    Brother mine, O brother !

Drive out the alien horde

    Brother mine, O brother !

With spear and glittering sword,

    Brother mine, O brother !

Cleanse the land from stain of sin,

Bring thine exiled people in,

Let the reign of Christ begin,

    Brother mine, O brother !

MARIE.

Like a shy flower is she—
　A flower of Palestine ;
As slender as the tall palm tree,
　As tender as the vine—
Her eyes are like the summer sea
　When the wistful waters shine.

I love to watch her face
　Whereon the sunlight plays ;
Her chair doth seem a hallowed place ;
　And when her finger strays
Adown the page the lines to trace,
　My heart in silence prays.

I watch her soft bright hair
　Whereon the sunlight shines,
I look to see a halo there

Where light the face enshrines :
I seem to hear a ghostly prayer,
  As her hand my flower entwines.

Her face is very pale—
  I sometimes see a tear :
I wonder does she sob and wail
  When none is by to hear ;
Her sorrow makes my spirit quail—
  My heart doth ache with fear.

I pray God comfort her,
  O poor lone aching heart !
I dare not speak, I dare not stir,
  We seem so far apart ;
She seems my silence to prefer—
  My voice doth make her start.

God knoweth which is best—

    She hath her lonely dreams :

And I perchance a life-long quest,

    That to her worthless seems :

Our barks that erewhile touched at rest

    Now float down separate streams.

And yet how can it be,

    That I must drift away ;

Her presence set my spirit free—

    She taught my soul to pray ;

Oh ! in some far eternity,

    We two shall find the day.

Our souls are groping yet

    In darkness of the night ;

Her eyes with many tears are wet—

For wrongs she cannot right ;

Her people's pain can she forget,

Or smile within my sight ?

I sometimes wonder where

Her radiant spirit dwells ;

Her body is so pure and fair,

And yet her soul rebels

And wings its flight to upper air

By strange mysterious spells.

Leaving the earthly frame—

The Spirit doth it seek ?

She hears not when I speak her name,

Her pulse is faint and weak.

From out the Ark of Heaven she came—

My dove so pale and meek.

E

Should she to Heaven return,

    What message could she take ?

My kiss on her white brows would burn

    With fire that nought could slake ;

My olive branch she will not spurn—

    Yea, wear it for my sake.

Only the olive bough

    That cries aloud for peace ;

Methinks her spirit hears me now

    And sighs for its release ;

My token green she will allow,

    Between us wars shall cease.

Thy Home in skies above

    Rebuild, O mourner ! here,

Teach us the height and depth thereof,

Show us the vision clear ;
Thou, who hast learned the ways of love,
    Draw love to us more near.

Teach us the angel song
    Thy spirit erst did sing
Ere thy pure soul, made sad by wrong,
    Had learned to droop its wing ;
Thy long tried patience made thee strong,
    We crave thy suffering.

Teach us by thy true woe
    That mourning shall be blest ;
Such mourning shall pure comfort know,
    Such sorrow shall find rest ;
Yea ! living streams of healing flow
    To mourners, east and west.

When mourning tears are dried.

Hail then earth's Easter morn ;

Humanity, long crucified,

From barren tomb reborn,

Shall know the Brother who once died

To free our race from scorn.

A Light to all the earth,

And Israel's glorious Crown—

His tomb shall give a nation birth.

His Kingdom gain renown ;

Joseph shall free the land from dearth.

And rebuild David's town.

O Bethlehem of Judea !

The little house of bread

Shall hold the remnant, feel no fear,

Thy children shall be fed ;

The nations come from far and near

Bowing to Christ the head.

O Judah's Bethlehem !

That shalt be callèd great ;

The star reveals the diadem,

Accept thy royal state ;

Thy crown, emblazoned gem by gem,

Thy God doth now create.

" Thou shalt also be a crown of glory in the hand of the Lord, and a royal diadem in the hand of thy God."—ISAIAH lxii.

" They shall be as the stones of a crown, lifted up as an ensign upon his land."—ZECHARIAH ix. 16.

EASTER DAWN.

CHRISTIAN AND JEW.

CHRISTIAN.

Hast thou seen Christ, brother, risen, crowned with
glory,

Coming in His Majesty to judge and to make war ?

Hast thou seen Christ, brother, Him of olden story,

Coming as the sun-god with steeds and flaming car ?

JEW.

Nay, nay, I saw Him not—

But this way came one day

A stranger, without purse or scrip,

Yet giving bread away.

CHRISTIAN.

Hast thou seen Christ, brother, risen in His splendor,

Crowned with crown of Solomon, the mild and peaceful
    king ?

Benignant is His countenance, His eyes serene and
    tender.

To Him the kings of all the earth their righteous tribute
    bring.

JEW.

Nay, nay, I saw Him not—

    But a beggar I have seen,

Who, when I clothed him with my cloak,

    Looked up with face serene.

CHRISTIAN.

Had'st thou seen Christ, brother, then in joy and
wonder,

Thy heart in very thankfulness would shout and sing
in praise,

For the Heaven that is above Him, and the deep that
lieth under,

Do join forever in that song throughout all nights and
days.

JEW.

Nay, nay, I've seen Him not—

But a child with wistful face,

That drank some water from my hand,

Looked back with loving grace.

CHRISTIAN.

And yet we both have seen Him, have seen Him, O
    my brother !

For was He not the Stranger who gave the hungry
    bread ?

And was He not the Beggar, and the Child ? indeed
    none other

Hast thou clothed and given water to, but Christ him
    to thee led.

JEW.

Nay, nay, I know Him not,

    But this I ever feel—

The needy must be cared for,

    Be it my woe or weal.

" Inasmuch as ye did it unto the least of these my little ones
ye did it unto me."

THREE ROSES.

Three roses bloom in Paradise—

    Three roses red are blooming there ;

The first a rose beyond all price,

    The second rose beyond compare,

And oh ! the sweetness of the last

Will live when all earth's joys are past.

THE BELOVÈD.

A pearl is my belovèd—

    A pearl from the restless sea :

God lifted her from the watery deeps,

    To give her soul to me :

And on my breast her spirit sleeps

    In silent ecstacy.

A flower is my belovèd—

    A lily white and fair :

Her hidden roots are in the earth,

    But her soul blooms in the air ;

My love hath given her soul re-birth,

    And her heart exhales in prayer.

A shrine is my belovèd—
  Where my tired soul kneels to pray.
A wanderer, without place of rest
  Was I,—no Sabbath day,
No house of God, no home, no nest,
  Till her heart said " loved one, stay."

A wind is my belovèd—
  That sweeps through my surging soul—
A wind, a breath from the lips of God ;
  Her word doth make me whole ;
And the almond blooms on Aaron's rod,
  And the waters backward roll.

A harp is my belovèd—
  A harp of a thousand strings ;
And when the soft south wind doth blow,
  Her soul vibrates and rings
With a song my heart sang long ago,
  And again my spirit sings.

A dove is my belovèd—
  A white-winged nestling dove ;
She floated long on the waters wide,
  Caged in the home of love ;
Now in my breast she doth abide,
  And the olive blooms above.

A star is my belovèd—
  A far off shining star ;
She lifts me from ethereal heights,
  To dwell where angels are ;
She teaches me all pure delights
  From out Heaven's golden bar.

A queen is my belovèd—
  A queen and a gentle child ;
Her calm eyes shine with holy love
  Power, veiled in aspect mild ;
She comforts me as comforting dove,
  And my heart is reconciled.

A bride is my belovèd—
  Bride of the Sacrifice ;
God hears her heart's continual prayer ;
  God meets her upturned eyes
With raptures sweet, and visions rare,
  And joys of Paradise.

O holy best belovèd—
  My pearl, my queen, my shrine,
My lily-flower, my harp of gold,
  My bride, whose bread and wine
Fills me with raptures new and old,
  And makes my life divine.

THE ELIJAH MINISTRY.

" Behold, I will send you Elijah the prophet before the coming of the great and dreadful day of the Lord : and he shall turn the heart of the fathers to the children, and the heart of the children to their fathers, lest I come and smite the earth with a curse."—MALACHI iv. 5-6.

" Intreat me not to leave thee, nor to return from following after thee : for whither thou goest, I will go ; and where thou lodgest, I will lodge : thy people shall be my people, and thy God my God :

" Where thou diest, will I die, and there will I be buried ; the Lord do so to me, and more also, if aught but death part thee and me."—RUTH i. 16-17.

THE PRAYER OF ELIJAH.

O Lord, my God, the heavens rend
And let the dove of peace descend
    Upon the cherished Bride.
Make her all glorious within :
Clothed with pure robes and cleansed from sin,
    Let her be justified.

The power of Thy redeeming Word
Within her lives ; Thy glittering sword
    In mercy sheathe awhile
Till men may learn to know her worth,
And, healed from sickness, pain, and dearth,
    Grow pure beneath her smile.

Long, by the streams of Babylon,
Hath she her mourning robes put on,
 Her harps on willows hung ;
Oh ! dry her sad repentant tears,
Assuage her griefs and calm her fears—
 Perfecting hath begun.

In sweetness and humility
She seeks to set the captives free—
 The outcasts bringing home ;
None is so poor but she will bend
To yield them grace, and succour lend
 Where Thy lost exiles roam.

None is so low but she will lift
Them up by her transcendent gift—
 The chalice of the spouse ;
By that mysterious marriage tie
The good shall live, the evil die ;
 O mighty men, arouse !

Arouse yourselves, ye exiled host !
The Lord, by power of Holy Ghost,
　　By water, and by flame,
Reveals His love to us again,
Reveals His goodness unto men ;
　　Blest be His glorious Name.

The Bride—now filled with deep desire
For love that, as consuming fire,
　　Shall purge away her stains—
Seeks to be perfect as her King ;
To her your righteous tribute bring ;
　　Her throne she now regains.

Crown with a crown our beauteous queen ;
Her glory in all lands be seen :
　　Her leaves the nations heal ;
Her marvellous faith—that did endure
The fires of hell to be made pure—
　　God's power doth now reveal.

O Israel's Queen—to exile driven,
Sustained by God with bread from Heaven
    Until the pregnant time—
Cried " Let the daughter be brought forth,
Hid in the darkness of the north,
    To her own land and clime."

Visions of God do now unseal
The prophecy ; O Bride reveal
    His wisdom unto men ;
With childlike voice, and childlike face,
With childlike heart, and simple grace,
    Sing Zion's songs again.

The harp of David dwells in thee,
With music shalt thou set us free ;
    Rebuild Jerusalem ;
Prophetic eyes shall soon declare
Thou art the Queen and Bride most fair,
    Made rich with many a gem.

Prophetic eyes shall hail the Bride

As one with Him, the crucified—

 Union with God complete;

Then shall men say " The Lord is there,"

Jehovah Shamnah shall declare

 His will in tones most sweet.

Prophetic eyes shall soon confess

She is " The Lord, our Righteousness,"

 Jehovah Tsidkenu ;

Then shall all wars and tumults cease,

Jehovah Shalom shall send peace

 From out the Heavens new.

THE SONG OF THE KING'S DAUGHTER.

The harp of God is in my hands.

I sing the songs of Zion,

Come, come ye outcasts from all lands,

Prevailed has Judah's Lion ;

Come to the banner that I hold—

Come, come ye weak and be made bold,

Lift up your silver and your gold—

The cross your God did die on.

The harp of God with music wakes,

And kings do bow before it ;

Triumphant love the silence breaks,

And lowly hearts adore it ;

Dawns now the resurrection morn ;

A nation from the dead re-born,

As from the barren tomb was torn

The King who shall restore it.

I am a child of Israel's race,
    Though into exile driven,
Now brought again to mine own place ;
    With wrestling angel striven,
As Israel, I have prevailed
When the accuser me assailed,
The powers of hell before me quailed
    By Word asunder riven.

Incarnate was that Word in me
    By Christ now re-created ;
The captive Word hath been set free,
    And Israel reinstated ;
Her marriage robes she may now don,
Her glorious crown may be put on,
Her exile past, her kingdom won,
    Her Bride and Bridegroom mated.

O mighty one of Israel ! thou

    Hast wrought this restoration ;

And unto Thee all men shall bow,

    Thou shepherd of the nation.

Thou stone, that shalt to pieces dash ;

Thou scourge, that shalt the nations lash ;

Thou thunder, and thou earthquake crash ;

    Begin the new creation.

Restore the virgin, once defiled,

    Condemned to robes of mourning ;

Then, Levi's cruelty reviled ;

    Now, Levi's love adorning,

Prepares the way before her feet,

Anoints with oil, and spices sweet,

Her head, and bids the nations greet

    A Queen above all scorning.

Dinah—the purging, judging word—
    Great Israel's only daughter
Made barren by harsh Levi's sword
    And Simeon's cruel slaughter,
By God again has been raised up;
Her hands now hold the holy cup—
The marriage feast where men may sup
    The wine Christ turns from water.

O holy chalice of the spouse
    In mercy long withholden,
Till the sole daughter of the house
    Could clásp that chalice golden,
And shelter in her virgin breast
The mystery yet unexpressed
By which all mankind shall be blest,
    Ordained from ages olden.

O holy Virgin, Queen, and Bride !

   When men, thy flesh revering,

Shall see in thee the crucified,

   Veiled in his new appearing ;

By risen flesh, the Bridegroom kind,

Again shall heal the sick and blind,

Set captives free, restore each mind

   That hath been weak and fearing.

The house of God is now with men ;

   Prepare the temple lowly,

The tabernacle build again,

   Receive the vision holy ;

He is our God, our day, our night,

He is our peace, He is our light,—

Yea, every eye shall see that sight,

   Though yet the dawn breaks slowly.

Woman, the temple of the Lord,
Shall hold the hidden treasure ;
In her, the purifying word
Shall soon reveal God's pleasure ;
When purged as with refining fire,
When held by magnet of desire,
Our sins before her touch expire,
Then joy shall know no measure.

Kneel, all ye sons of Levi, kneel !
A voice doth rend the heaven,
And visions shall to you reveal
The word in mercy given ;
When Israel's house is built once more,
The King shall to each son restore
The portion that he held of yore,
Before the House was riven.

Build your waste places, child and queen,
   Restore the broken-hearted,
Lead them by streams in valleys green ;
   Bind friends whom grief hath parted ;
Let peace like a great river flow ;
Let lilies in the meadows grow ;
In desert sands let roses blow ;
   The tender shoots have started.

Under your all-embracing love
   That yearns for man's perfecting,
Feeling with Saviour God above,
   The smart of sin's rejecting.
One with the sinner and the slain,
One with the great Redeemer's pain,—
O blessed Bride, your joy regain
   By faith, the all-expecting.

Let faith and hope and love conspire—
A threefold cord is binding—
To give to thee thy heart's desire :
Through devious pathways winding
The scattered Levites to thee come ;
Build them again in their own home ;
From Him they never more shall roam,
Through thee their portion finding.

Joined to the Lord shall Levi be,
Inheriting his blessing ;
Dead is the sin of cruelty,
His Master's Cross confessing :
The Holy One shall be revealed,
The Godly mystery be unsealed,
The nation joined, the breach be healed ;
O rapture past expressing.

SUB SILENTIO.

II.

My words can never tell

The love I feel for thee ;

Let silence speak,

Nor break the holy spell ;

My words too faint, too weak,

Sound like a silver bell;

In golden silence dwell

Apart from me.

When the last trump shall wake

The prisoned dead,

Then may I silence break ;

Then, on thy head,

O love! may I outpour

In blessings all the store

Of love unspoken now;

Then, on thy spotless brow,

Which all men shall adore,

May I a crown display;

Then, on that happy day,

Sing, as I sang before,

Praises to thy dear eyes.

Praise to thy heart,

Praises to all thou art

In Paradise!

A MESSAGE.

Bring me no roses till the tears are dried

   In sorrowing eyes that weep in grief alone ;

Bring me no kisses ; call me not thy bride—

   Behold, thou can'st not make a bride of stone,

And stony griefs are mine while others weep ;

While others watch. shall I take rest in sleep ?

   Nay, nay, thou can'st not for these woes atone.

Weave me no chaplet for my aching brows ;

   Bring me no blessings yet of corn and wine ;

If thou wilt call me sister, friend, or spouse,

   Then lend thine aid to make the earth divine ;

If thou dost love me. I do charge thee—go.

And to the poorest, love and pity show ;

   From their reflected light my face shall shine.

Pour out thy love upon the poor oppressed,

So shall I know thou truly lovest me,

For every smile thou bring'st on face distressed,

Upon my face mirrored that smile shall be ;

And if a sad and sinning wretch ye find,

Oh ! speak him fair, entreat with words most kind,

Uplifting him, my soul shall rise more free.

Bring me no words of love, however sweet,

Lest siren music lull my soul to rest ;

But oh ! a thousand times those words repeat

Unto the weary heart and aching breast ;

Believing I with them thy comforting share,

To know that comfort I their griefs will bear,

And I, in them, by thee shall still be blest.

A thousand times more blest than when love takes

    Love to itself alone ; if love be true,

Thou wilt but hold me dearer for their sakes

    To whom I give you now, and them to you—

A thousand hearts shall thus rejoice for one,

And all good deeds to them for me be done,

    And in their joy my joy shall live anew.

Thus human love our souls shall ever bind

    In union blest and sweet though never seen ;

We'll love the world, together, with one mind ;

    God and the world, then, what can come between ?

A chain of love thus link by link we'll make—

Kind words, kind deeds for our Belovèd's sake,

    Till all earth's hearts shall know His peace serene.

AN ANSWER.

Perchance, belovèd, thou wilt never know

   On earth, the love my heart hath given to thee?

   There is no music, in the rhythmèd sea,

That can my melody divinest show;

There is no word, in any winds that blow,

   To speak the fulness of my ecstacy;

   Words would but bind my soul whose currents free

From myriad radiates to their centre flow.

My harp is dumb before thee—if it strove

   To speak in music of thy hallowed face,

Its thousand strings would all unequal prove

   To set love forth; the passion of my race

Encloses thee and sets thee far above

   All earthly love upon God's throne of Grace.

MY SABBATH.

"There remaineth a rest for the people of God."

The days are always sabbath days
    On which thou com'st to me ;
My heart awakes with songs of praise,
    Mine eyes clear visions see ;
And, for the humblest of our race,
I plead before the Throne of Grace.

The days are days of heavenly rest,—
    My weary heart seems still ;
Shall not His holy presence blest
    The sanctuary fill ?
Shall not His cloud of glory shine
From out the inmost holiest shrine?

The days are days of hallowed peace ;
A holy dove doth brood ;
He bids my sad complaining cease—
From evil cometh good ;
And oh ! the darkness of my night
With starry splendour is made bright.

O days of peace ! O days of rest !
O days of fresh new joy !
Upon the ever-faithful breast,
Our bliss knows no alloy ;
Beneath the everlasting arm,
We sleep secure from fear or harm.

THE UNSPOKEN WORD.

We know, but dare not speak, for where are ears
   To hear the melodies that forth would break,
   If once again the silver trumpet spake,
Declaring—He shall wipe away all tears;
That death and hell, captivity's long years,
   Are swallowed up in victory? Oh, awake!
   Come from your graves, lost Israel! forsake
Your idols, Ephraim; lo! your God appears!
Look and behold the loved of every eye,
   Desire of every nation, king of men;
As chaff before the whirlwind, sin shall fly,
   And fire shall lick the stubble up again;
As silver, He shall purge and purify
   The sons of Levi, bring the captives ten.

THE SONG OF JUDAH.

"All flesh is grass, and all the goodliness thereof is as the flower of the field :

"The grass withereth, the flower fadeth : because the Spirit of the Lord bloweth upon it : surely the people is grass.

" The grass withereth, the flower fadeth : but the word of our God shall stand forever."—ISAIAH xl.

" For this is life eternal : to know Thee, the only true God, and Jesus Christ whom Thou hast sent."

Withers the grass of man's desire :

Withers the woman's flower-like face ;

Like dross consumed on a burning pyre,

Each form returns to its own last place,

Ashes to ashes, and dust to dust ;

Is there treasure in heaven, nor moth, nor rust

Can consume ? incorrupt as the flame of fire ?

Surely the people are but as grass;

When the spirit blows, they shall fade away;

Like flowers of the field they do bloom, and pass

Back to the earth and the mire of clay!

Fading and passing and changing all,

To the shadowy land beyond recall;

Is it long night there, or an endless day?

A shadow, a vapour, a breath is life;

Have I lived and moved? do I live, or dream?

Am I a part of the endless strife,

Or a shadow with shadows that only seem?

Once did I find in a woman's face,

The dream of my life, with a dream's sweet grace?—

It flickers and fades like a sunset gleam.

Pale as a lily, and wan and white—

　Was she a woman or fading flower?

She bloomed and she died in a single night—

　What can avail to destroy death's power?

Is there a land of fadeless bloom?

Is there a life beyond the tomb?

　Is there aught but the passing hour?

O lily and rose, are you blooming yet

　In the sweet, dim garden we used to know?

With the dews of night is your pale cheek wet?

　Are the spices sweet? Do the apples grow?

Do the ring-doves coo in the listening trees?

Do the roses ope to the southern breeze?

　And my kiss of love—doth it bud and blow?

O Lord, my God, Thine Almighty Hand

  Alone can save from the woe and waste ;

Thy Word, my God, shall forever stand ;

  Let my parching lips of Thy waters taste ;

Are there streams eternal for man to find ?

Are we dead in sin ? Are our eyes made blind ?

  O heal us, Belovèd, in haste ! in haste !

O Thou, the Eternal and only One,

  Who for us hath vanquished the barren tomb ;

When our life in death is over and done,

  In Thy risen beauty new life shall bloom

As fadeless lilies, in Thee we rise

As morning stars—we shall fill the skies ;

  The seed of the faithful re-born from gloom.

Thou who created'st the sun and stars—

What is man that Thou mindest him ?

Can he set Thee limits, or make Thee bars ?

Can he add to Thy glory ? or make it dim ?

Thou art the essence of glory and light ;

Can he make Thee dark ? can he make Thee bright ?

Can he fashion himself in a single limb ?

Nay, Thou hast made us—Thy sons are we—

Made us to shine as the stars are set

To witness Thy glory ; we come forth free—

The hidden and exiled we waked and met

As brothers long parted—we met to find

A single thought in the dual mind,

And a coal on the altar was glowing yet.

There is kinship in spirit, in soul, in blood ;

    The cloudy phantoms forever flee ;

Love is not drowned by the water flood,

    Nay, from the water she rises free ;

Love is not drowned, nay, my sister fair,

In the dim old garden we find her there,

    And the apples grow on the old green tree.

Sister, sweet sister, with eyes of dove,

    In the clefts of rock thou didst long abide ;

O tender-hearted ! O dear lost love !

    Why didst thou leave me so long to hide ?

Why were we sundered who are not twain ?

O gentle heart, thou art mine again—

    Mine forever, whate'er betide.

Come, dear heart, to thy garden green—,

   The lilies bloom and the roses wait ;

Come to thy people, O dear lost queen !

   All thy beauties we'll celebrate—

Praise to thy lips, and thine hair, and thine eyes,

Praise to thy low-voiced sweet replies,

   Thy gentle mien, and thy royal state.

Would I not crown thee with jewels bright ;

   Clothe thee in silver and cloth of gold ?

O my dove with the wings so white !

   O my pearl which I clasp and hold !

Lily, re-risen from barren tomb—

Christ's own lily—come forth and bloom,

   Bloom forever in all men's sight.

O daughter of Zion ! the chosen race

   Claims thee, fair daughter, to be its own ;

The God of our fathers, in mercy and grace,

   Builded thy walls of the jasper stone ;

Thy walls are salvation, thy gates are praise ;

Riches and honour, and length of days

   Are with thee who art builded by God alone.

Yea, he has fashioned thee, daughter fair ;

   Raised thee up from thy low estate ;

Binds bright gems in thy lustrous hair ;

   Bids the virgins upon thee wait.

Thou shalt find favour in all men's eyes—

Bride of the symbol of sacrifice—

   Little one, yet to be callèd great.

O little child, thou art God's great gift

   Unto His people, all shall be blessed,

All whom by mercy thou can'st uplift—

   Sad and sorrowful, weak, distressed ;

For Joseph's blessing in thee revives,

And thy garnered grain saves many lives ;

   God's love to His people, in thee expressed.

Dumb is my heart, when I fain would speak—

   Dumb with delight, O thou child so wise ;

Full is my heart, though my words are weak,

   In wonder and awe death's pale phantom dies,

For the sun glows brighter because of thee.

And the bubbling waters dance for glee,

   In lowly valleys the lilies rise.

Myriad harps could not sing my joy ;

  How can one feeble voice express

The fulness of rapture without alloy ?

  Oh ! many tongues should thy worth confess ;

Multitudes, multitudes shout and sing

The joy that thou find'st in thy risen King ;

  But let me sing of thy tenderness.

Nay, nay, but I'll ever silence keep—

  Golden silence for me is blest ;

Hide me away in a deep sweet sleep,

  Hide me away with thee to rest ;

What God knoweth, man cannot know ;

What God doeth, man cannot show ;

  His ways are hidden, He knoweth best.

MY LADY'S BOWER.

Oh, once my lady called me to her bower—
  A hallowed place, made dark by leafy screen,
  The softened sunlight filtered through the green
Cool shady leaves ; no painter hath the power
To picture her ; I knelt one passing hour,
  And wished that it eternity had been ;
  So gracious was her look and gentle mien,
To give my life had been too poor a dower ;
What had I done to merit her sweet gaze ?
  My heart, abashed, was dumb, my thought she read,
And so consoled me with sweet words of praise,
  And laid her gentle hand upon my head,—
And oh ! methought her hand had power to raise
  My soul to life e'en had it long been dead.

THE SONG OF SONGS.

THE BRIDEGROOM.

Open thy heart, my dove, open to me
  Thy tender leaves sweet flower, made for delight,
I would that all mankind might with me see
  Thy pure, bright soul, so spotless and so white ;
Art thou a lily flower ? or art a rose ?
A double fragrance from thy centre flows,
  And spicy odours fill the airs of night.

Open, my sister, loved one undefiled—
  My locks are heavy with the falling dews ;
Open, beloved one ; O my pleasant child,
  Hearing my voice, can'st thou my love refuse ?
" My coat is off, how shall I put it on ? "
I opened, but my own beloved was gone—
  " Oh ! can ye bring me of him any news ? "

THE DAUGHTERS and THE BRIDE.

" Oh ! what is thy belovèd ? woman fair ;

    Is thy belovèd more than other one ? "

" Yea, my belovèd is beyond compare,

    Loveliest of the lovely, he alone

Can enter in behind the wicket gate ;

He whom my soul doth love, tarry not late !

    Oh ! tell me, daughters, where my love hath gone.

" His curling locks are like the raven's black ;

    His eyes are eyes of doves, and fitly set ;

His lips, like lilies, no sweet spices lack.

    I charge you, daughters, if ye him have met,

I charge you go and tell my lovely friend

I faint for love ; bid him his footsteps wend

    Thither, for, oh ! my heart doth languish yet.

" My loved one is to me and I to him ;

Among the lilies there his soul doth feed ;

In his sweet garden, where the twilight dim

Doth hallow with its shade the sultry need ;

There doth he linger 'midst the beds of spice,

There doth his beauty all my soul entice ;

Yea, for my love his loveliness doth plead."

THE PEOPLE.

"O Shulamite ! O Shulamite ! return !

Return ! return ! that we may look on thee ;

For thy sweet beauty all our hearts do burn."

" But in the Shulamite what will ye see ? "

"A company of camps, two armies great,

Singers and dancers, princes of the state,

The willing chariots of my people free."

Who putteth forth her beauty as the morn,

Fair as the moon, and than the sun more bright ;

Her banners do an army great adorn —

An army gathered for victorious fight ;

Upon thy neck the shields shall hang again ;

A thousand bucklers—shields of mighty men,

A chosen army held by Love's great might.

THE BRIDEGROOM.

Thou art all fair, my love ; thou art all fair,

My lily among thorns, no spot in thee ;

To thy pure beauty what can I compare ?—

A company of horsemen shall I see ?

And banners gleaming bright with many a gem ?

Comely as Tirzah and Jerusalem—

Of gold and silver shall thy borders be.

THE BRIDE.

I am a wall, my breasts are like strong towers—

Therefore have I found favour and sweet peace;

Assail me, if ye will, ye thunderous powers,

My wall shall make your stormy battles cease:

Give all the substance of your house for love,

Yet ever insufficient will it prove—

My love can make a thousand loves increase.

THE BRIDEGROOM.

" Set me a seal, my love, upon thy heart ;

Set me a seal, my love, upon thine arm ;

For jealousy hath a most cruel smart—

There is no voice, however sweet, can charm

Away the coals which are as coals of fire,

A vehement flame ; O ! Bride of my desire !

Love, strong as death, shall shield thee from all harm.

" Love, strong as death, which floods can never drown,

Nor many waters quench ; O ceaseless flame !

My risen sun shall nevermore go down,

When multitudinous voices speak thy name ;

Who cometh forth from desert with delight,

Leaning on her beloved in all men's sight ? "—

" The Bride, whose towers and banners overcame."

THE CHILD BRIDE.

"He that is mighty hath magnified me, and Holy is His Name."

"And of Levi he said, Let thy Thummin and thy Urim be with thy holy one, whom thou didst prove at Massah, and with whom thou didst strive at the waters of Meribah;

"Who said unto his father and to his mother, I have not seen him ; neither did he acknowledge his brethren, nor knew his own children ; for they have observed thy word, and kept thy covenant.

"They shall teach Jacob thy judgments, and Israel thy law : they shall put incense before thee, and whole burnt sacrifice upon thine altar.

"Bless, Lord, his substance, and accept the work of his hands ; smite through the loins of them that rise against him, and of them that hate him, that they rise not again."

DEUTERONOMY xxxiii. 8-9-10-11.

THE SONS OF KOHATH.

"The service of the sanctuary belonging unto them was that they should bear it upon their shoulders."—NUMBERS vii. 9.

In far-off heavenly places,

Like a star, my soul is set

To learn celestial graces,

And earthly woes forget ;

Let the robes of Heaven me cover,

And adorn me for my lover ;

Let my heart know no regret.

Thou hast lifted me to Heaven,

And returned again to men,

And a sceptre to me given.

To rule the hidden ten ;

This has been thy heart's deep pleasure—

To restore the hidden treasure,

And rebuild the House again.

O brother ! when I'm sitting

  On my throne within the sky,

Where my Saviour-God, is fitting

  Me for that place most high,

I shall hear thy prayers ascending,

Like incense to me wending—

  And my prayers shall make reply.

If I leave thee in the garden,

  My love, for a little while ;

Forgive me, love, and pardon,

  If my heart did thee beguile ;

But the fires of God me sifted,

And thine own strong wings me lifted

  To live beneath God's smile.

There my heart can know no sorrow;

　There mine eyes can weep no tears;

There is no night nor morrow,

　Nor days, nor months, nor years,

But only bliss supernal,

And joy, and life eternal,

　Where the smile of God appears.

I am the little sister

　Thou hast borne upon thy breast;

Thou hast carried her and kissed her,

　And brought her into rest;

And the little one so lowly

Shall be callèd great and holy,

　As the Virgin Mother blest.

THE KNOWLEDGE OF THE LORD.

When earth is filled with knowledge of the Lord,

As the wide waters cover now the sea ;

When risen peoples, by His Word set free,

Shall drink full measure of the life restored,

Beating their pruning hooks from cruel sword,

Living, each man, beneath his own fig tree,

Where none can meddle with his liberty,

Nor with true worship to his God adored ;

Oh ! then, perchance, we may, in calm delight,

View the wide scene where splendor is displayed,.

And gaze on starry wonders of the night,

With nought to trouble us or make afraid ;

Beholding Him with our own mortal sight ;

Beholding Him and being not dismayed.

THE NEW SONG.

The universal woman counseleth her lover to find in nature symbols of eternal love.

She prophesieth of the hidden Word that shall be brought forth; of Wisdom's restraining powers; of the Mercies of God; of the removal of the curse through the sacrificial use of the Bride.

She speaks, as the Bride, of the hidden nature of Wisdom; of the union of earth with heaven in spousal mystery: the fruits of that union—a new heavens and a new earth, wherein dwelleth righteousness.

Two currents, rushing, mad with deafening roar;

Two waves that leap, and falling, kiss the shore;

Two birds that higher, and ever higher, soar.

Two stars, revolving in the empyrean blue;

Two stars of splendor, old, yet ever new;

These be the answer of my heart to you.

For what are words, and tones, and songs, and sighs?

And what are kisses and low-voiced replies?—

But shadows of a love that speaks and dies.

And what are suns, and stars, and seas, and sands?

And what are rushing streams and spreading lands?—

But symbols of the love that understands.

And multitudinous voices must reply

To hearts that sound the universal cry ;

And echoes speak in tones that cannot die.

And multitudinous voices must restrain

The Word, that spoken once, comes not again,

Lest that dread Word should flood the world with pain.

In love and fear 'tis given—in fear and love

Must we receive that blessing from above,

That shall the earth and heaven together move.

O holy priests and prophets of the Lord,

When that unspoken Word shall be restored,

Then God shall be in every heart adored.

Then from the earth shall sons of God come forth ;

Then tidings glad make light the darkened north ;

For God is not for ever with us wroth.

He doth but punish us a little while,

'Till sin be purged ; then wreathes the radiant smile,

And flowers do bloom in hearts made free from guile.

Flows now His mercy from the Throne of Grace ;

Smiles, once again, the all benignant face ;

And roses bloom in Israel's desert place.

Flows now His mercy forth like corn, and wine,

And oil ; O blessings from the Hand Divine,

God give me grace to take and make you mine.

With goodness Thou dost satiate my soul,

Like oil adown my head Thy blessings roll ;

I yield myself, O God, to Thy control.

O overshadowing power, I do not quake!

Thy Word, that shall the earth and heavens shake,

I'll hear, and bear, and utter for Thy sake.

Stupendous Word that doth my weak flesh bow,

Yet Word that lifts the curse from every brow,

To purest sacrifice, myself I vow.

Yet sacrifices burnt, Thou wouldest not ;

In mercy Thou hast cleansed from every spot—

A body without blemish, stain, or blot.

Lo! in the volume it is written there ;

I come to do Thy Will—a body fair ;

Hast fitted me—I come Thy cross to bear.

I come to bear the cross in risen life,

To speak the word that heals the world from strife ;

The Lamb's own symbol—hidden Bride and wife.

The sacrificial use in marriage tie;

I live by Him, who for my life did die,

My lovely one—desired of every eye.

Only the wise can hear and understand;

Only the good can find that promised land;

Only the true be fed by love's own hand.

O Lord, my heart in adoration bends,

The sacrifice of praise it upwards sends,

As heaven with earth, and earth with heaven, blends.

To God the Father, now, and God the Son,

And God the Spirit—holy Three in One—

Be uttered with one voice " Thy Will be done."

In love and fear, united Holy Name—

In fear and love, O sacrificial flame—

Descend, O wondrous Word that overcame.

Lord, let Thy glory, Thy Shekinah, shine

From out the holy place, the inner shrine ;

Let human life contain the life divine.

Live in the centre, Lord, and every part,

Control the mind, the will, the soul, the heart,

Let temples lowly hold Thee as Thou art.

Veiled in the flesh again let Godhead be—

Veiled in the flesh, the glorious Trinity ;

And knowledge of the Lord, like covering sea,

Fill all the earth with waves of majesty.

O WONDROUS EYES!

The individual woman entereth the sphere of the Bride, and becometh conscious of the individualizing love of the Spouse.

O wondrous eyes! O eyes of wondrous love!
  When thou dost look on me, my heavenly spouse,
  What deeps and deeps of love thou dost arouse!
Soul, heart, and mind, and strength, within me move
With one desire—that my whole life may prove
  The joy of loving Thee; enter my house,
  O heavenly guest! and let me crown Thy brows
With olive boughs, brought hither by the dove.
Dost Thou crown me? then, lowly at Thy feet,
  I sit in silence, gentlest, lovliest friend;
The odours of thy spikenard, smelling sweet,
  Unto my humble dwelling, fragrance lend;
Thy presence maketh all things fair and meet;
  Thy glories to my lowly heart descend.

THE LILY OF THE FIELD.

The individual woman findeth pleasure in humble duties as done unto her Spouse.

In the simplest, lowliest duty
Let me find, O Christ, Thy beauty,
  Nor the least of these despise,—
So shall I be a lily,
Growing so pure and stilly
  In the vales of Paradise.

I will bloom amid the grasses;
When my shepherd-lover passes,
  He will breathe my fragrant sighs,
And lift unto his bosom
The little, lowly blossom
  From the vales of Paradise.

I dreamed of starry splendor,
But my loved one said " surrender,"
  And quick my heart replies;
For the stars are dust before Thee,
And can stars and worlds adore Thee
  More than flowers of Paradise?

For the flowers do show the graces
That grow in heavenly places;
  And the blossoms of the skies
Put forth in petals airy
Star-forms, that unseen fairy
  Re-forms in Paradise.

Were I a star of Heaven—
One of the starry seven—
  I would live in my loved one's eyes;
Were I an earthly blossom,
I would fade upon his bosom,
  And re-bloom in Paradise.

TWO VISIONS.

Thine eyes the beauty and the glory see,

   And mine the darkness and the desolation,

The earthquake, and the gloom of Calvary

   From which was born again this new creation;

Oh! when shall men look on Thee—Israel's King;

When shall the nations righteous tribute bring,

   And praise and crown Thee God of our salvation?

When waves of glorious light about Thee shine,

   And opened eyes behold God's revelation,

Will not men bow before the Man Divine?—

   Light of the Gentiles, glory of His nation;

When rippling waves of phosphorescent seas

Break into chords of molten harmonies,

   Will not all hearts bow down in adoration?

Will not men know the heights and depths of love,

   Its lowly service and its risen glory?

Will they not drink, with joy, deep draughts thereof,

   Reserved for us throughout the ages hoary?

Will not the monsters 'neath the troubled waves—

Will not the dragons of the deeps and caves—

   Move, thrilled with joy, to hear the glad old story?

Will not the deep, that coucheth down below—

   Will not the choirs, in highest exaltation—

Shout with one voice, till earth and heaven shall know

   The meaning of that awful acclamation?

When He shall come, who is our Righteousness,

Then deeps below and heights above shall bless,

   And heaven and earth be joined in glad relation.

The trembling earth, vibrating, now doth quake ;

   The heavens with life new and unseen are thrilling ;

The thunder-crash, that heaven and earth shall shake,

   Comes with the Word, the righteous oath fulfilling,

The Word that makes alive, the Word that saves ;

O Israel, awake ! rise from your graves !

   His power shall come upon a people willing.

Come, in the beauty of Thy holiness,

   With dew of youth from out the womb of morning ;

Turn us again, O Lord ! redeem and bless

   The people Thou didst once condemn to scorning ;

Turn us again, O Lord ! we shall be turned,

And daily, incense on Thine altar burned ;

   The Bride be clothed with robes of love's adorning.

In visions of the Bride all men shall see

   The sacrifice divine—supreme surrender;

When oath of God shall make the people free,

   And flood the earth with Christ's ethereal splendor,

No heart so vile, so low, but quickening thrill

Shall tame its pulse and bend it to His Will—

   None can resist God's smile, serene and tender.

O Love! the all-pervading, quickening fire

   That promises new life and restoration;

Woman, who holds the magnet of desire,

   Beloved of all, sought for by every nation;

Woman, who holds the sacred spousal cup,

Shall, by the Spouse divine, be lifted up,

   'Till earth, prepared, becomes her habitation.

THE HARP OF DAVID.

Am I divinely mad, that I do dream

    That death is swallowed up in victory ?

    Oh ! am I mad, that do these visions see ?—

Peace flowing like a broad and swelling stream—

Disease, and crime, and woe, before it seem

    To vanish ; and the peoples, risen free—

    Under the perfect law of liberty—

The land, the chosen land, reclaim, redeem ;

Methought that David's harp in me lay still,

    And that the king struck all its chords again ;

It waked, and trembled with a sudden thrill,

    Cried out for joy, and then sobbed back with pain,

As sound and sense receded.   Oh ! fulfil

    The vision—David ! wake the frozen strain !

THE BRIDE.

My body and my blood to Christ are given ;
   Be it to me as my own Saviour wills,
E'en though the nails in quivering flesh be driven
   By traitorous hand, that kisses while it kills ;
Nay, by my own belovèd am I slain,
He wills that I should bear this deepest pain,
   His hand, the hand adored, that my blood spills.

The sacrifice of trembling flesh, while living,
   Did they not spurn and lash with cruel scourge ?
And shall I quiver if the self-same giving
   Pierces my heart and turns my song to dirge ?
And each red rose becomes a piercing thorn ?
And harps that sang of joy begin to mourn ?
   Oh ! let their weeping, cruel Levi purge.

Hide me away, O Christ, with Thee in heaven,

  Hide me with Thee, away from sight of men ;

The number of Thy bleeding wounds was seven,

  And must I make that number up again ?

Let this last cup pass from me, O my Lord,

Or let me die beneath the slayer's sword ;

  Shall I not be with Thee in glory then ?

Oh ! let thy brooding wings me close and cover ;

  This earth of thorns and briars I may not tread,—

That holds no love, that holds no righteous lover ;

  They cast my soul among the waking dead,

They cast my soul before death's mighty shade ;

Thy love, thy own betrothed, they have betrayed,

  And dust and ashes heaped upon her head.

Among the shades of death the night is blinding;

In chill and darkness, clouds and gathering gloom,

With groping hands, and staggering feet, I'm finding

The way to rise from out this prison tomb,

And lifting, slowly, eyes unused to light,

Lest they be blinded by the sudden sight

Of glorious sunshine and a land of bloom.

Darkness and doubt ?   Nay, but the clouds are shifting,

My prison walls with sudden glory shine,

And distant harps I hear, and voices, lifting

Their tones in praises of the gift divine,

And, oh ! their comforting doth soothe my pain,

My soul forgets it lies amongst the slain,

And Christ revives me with His bread and wine.

Revived, refreshed, renewed by love's own tending,

    I patiently regain the barren earth ;

Amongst the flowers again my way I'm wending,

    And peace and plenty banish woe and dearth ;

Ye cannot slay uninjurable love—

Revived by God it rushes from above,

    And, from its anguish, gains a higher birth.

Ye cannot slay ; but, oh ! the spirit's grieving,

    When ye, with impious hand, do seize the gift ;

Be sure the wakened soul knows no deceiving,

    The searching punishment is sure and swift ;

Why do ye thorns upon my forehead press

When I have come to give you tenderness,

    And, by my love, the lowly to uplift ?

Upon your knees, to God be ever praying,

   Lest nature, unredeemed, return the curse;

Lest, by your kiss, again the Son betraying,

   Base silver—price of blood—do fill your purse.

Too late, too late will be your sad repenting—

Cast out from love, there will be no relenting,

   And your last state than first will then be worse.

UNEXPRESSED.

By breathing of low lutes, by soft winds' sighing
  Gently among the frailest, tenderest flowers,
By dreams of azure in far sunsets dying,
  By pattering of warm, refreshing showers,
By Nature's kindliest moods—I would express
My wells of joy, my springs of tenderness.

By quietly flowing streams, serenely gliding
  Through placid meadows gemmed with starry flowers,
By blue forget-me-nots in grasses hiding,
  By lilies sheltered in cool fragrant bowers,
By all calm things of earth—I would redress
My words that breathe of aught but tenderness.

My heart is filled, oh ! filled to overflowing,

   All words do fail ; breathes, in the tender flowers,

Some hint of all my love, past earthly showing,

   That blooms eternal, now, in heavenly bowers ;

Let songs of earth, and choirs of heaven, confess

There is no voice to speak Love's tenderness.

Part III.

THE CASTLE OF THE SOUL.

K

"The soul of the just man is nothing less than a Paradise in which God finds his delight."—ST. TERÉSA.

THE HOLY OF HOLIES.

Thy soul reached out unto my soul,
    I saw their arms entwine—
One being—pure, complete, and whole,
    Re-formed by power divine ;
Above the holy dove did brood,
And, in that dual solitude,
    The face of God did shine,

And, lo ! the vision changed again—
    I saw a temple fair,
Translucent, white, freed from all stain,
    Floating in lambent air,
And every sweet and holy thought
Within its traceries was wrought
    By love's continual prayer.

O brother mine, how pure a thing
Is a white virgin soul—
A palace for a royal king
To hold in sweet control;
Our hearts shall be His willing throne,
There let Him dwell and reign alone,
While the long seasons roll.

Perpetual peace, perpetual joy,
And everlasting rest;
No cares of earth can there annoy
The slumbers of the blest;
He giveth His belovèd sleep,
Angels have charge their souls to keep
On the eternal breast.

I would not dream, I would not wake,
  I do not care to see
What shall be, when this sleep shall break ;
  Lost in divinity
Gold shall refine from earthly dross ;
Life fill the measure of death's loss
  In love's eternity.

Equal shall be our pain and bliss ;
  Equal our calm and care :
Each wound be healed by gentle kiss ;
  Desire fulfilled by prayer ;
Our rapture silenced by our peace ;
Captivity shall mean release
  To hearts that enter there.

Silence! oh, silence! speak no word,

    And make no single sign;

Hush every breath, no air hath stirred

    That solitude divine—

Where death is swallowed up in life,

Where peace o'ershadows every strife,

    Closed in the cloudy shrine.

THE SONG OF HOLY REST.

When I give thee, then I hold thee;

   When I leave thee, I am nearest;

When another heart doth fold thee,

   Then I, smiling, whisper " dearest ";

When some weary heart doth bless thee,

Then, indeed, my lips caress thee,

   Then mine eyes shine on thee clearest.

When I love thee, then I yield thee,

   Then my soul doth whisper " brother ";

When another heart doth shield thee,

   With my heart I bless that other;

When in dreary path I find thee,

Then in loving bands I bind thee

   To thy duty, as a mother.

That I love thee—oh! believe me—

  Love thy soul as priceless treasure,

And that love shall ne'er deceive thee

  With the pale white shade of pleasure;

On a throne of joys I'll place thee,

And with gems immortal grace thee,

  There thy bliss shall know no measure.

Flowers in lowliest meads shall tell thee

  That thy lady hath passed thither;

Lonely nights of prayer compel thee

  To cry out "Oh! where and whither?"

But at last she shall enfold thee,

In her heart of hearts shall hold thee,

  When her sweet lips whisper "hither."

I will find thee when I loose thee,

Hold thee close, oh, tender-hearted !

Yea, above all things, shall choose thee—

Thou and I were too long parted ;

Now, at last, sweet love hath found thee,

And in gentle fetters bound thee ;

Healed the wounds that long had smarted.

When I leave thee I will bless thee ;

And by night, in visions holy,

Shall white wings of dove caress thee,

Make thy heart like manger lowly—

Holy shrine where love may take thee

When all earthly joys forsake thee,

When the passing bell tolls slowly.

O my loved one, thou dost send me,
    And I go, by thee made purer,
And thy wingèd prayers attend me,
    While, with nobler tread and surer,
I return to paths of duty,
Clothed with thy celestial beauty—
    Charity, the great endurer.

O strong heart that dost compel me
    To seek out the hidden treasure;
O strong lips, that dare to tell me
    Death can crown with crown of pleasure;
O strong words that onward drive me,
Priestly lips that cleanse and shrive me,
    Pouring blessings without measure.

O strong heart, that dost retrieve me

  All my griefs and all my losses;

Love supreme, that dost relieve me

  Of my burdens and my crosses;

Lo! thy sabbath days restore me,

And the peace of God flows o'er me;

  Ark, at rest, no longer tosses.

Rest of God thou art unto me;

  Take my heart within thy keeping,—

Lest the tempests wild undo me,

  Guard it in its holy sleeping;

Thou with tenderest love didst bless me,

And thy dove-like wings caress me,

  When my lonely eyes are weeping.

Oh! the joy of having known thee—

Blest remembrance leave me never;

Oh! the bliss of having shown thee

Love that lives and smiles forever;

In all things I now may trace thee,

Holy rest, and ever place thee

Where from me can nought thee sever.

Holy Rest, shine ever through me,

Blessing every human creature;

Holy, Heavenly Rest, renew me,

Beam with light in every feature;

Lamp of God forever light me,

With unflickering flame invite me

To the Sabbath Day of Nature.

Holy Rest, do not forsake me,

　When, with weary feet, I'm wending

Devious ways; oh! then re-take me,

　With thyself my being blending,—

Ever let thy deep soul rest me,

And with smiles will I invest thee,

　Smiles on rippling waters sending.

Smiles of joy beam ever on thee,

　All thy pain away beguiling;

Rest of God, descend upon me,

　Where my soul sits, ever smiling;

Oh! my God doth new create me;

And to heaven doth love translate me,

　With sweet words of comfort wiling.

Comforting Rest flows all around me

   Like soft summer seas, that, flowing,

With their gentle waves surround me,

   While my tresses, backward blowing,

Lie on water's breast,—I lay me

Where kind unseen arms convey me,

   Floating where my heart is going.

How can tempest dark assail me

   On this blue ethereal water?

Such pure love can never fail thee;

   "God hath made him thine, O daughter!"

" Yea, the winds and waves do love me,

With the smile of God above me;"

   " And the Rest her God hath brought her."

MAGNIFICAT.

"My soul doth magnify the Lord: and my spirit hath rejoiced in God my Saviour.

"For he hath regarded the lowliness of his handmaiden.

"For, behold, from henceforth all generations shall call me blessed.

"For he that is mighty hath magnified me, and holy is his name."

Thou lov'st my spirit, sailing far away

    Amid blue seas and isles of glorious stars;

Thou lov'st my soul, that lives in shining day

    Of God's delight, and knows no bonds nor bars;

And oh! methinks thou lov'st my body, too,

And eyes, where spirit shines and soul pours through;

    Since God hath healed sin's wounds and sorrow's scars.

What imperfections in me yet remain,

   He shall, too, purge, and make me worthier friend ;

And we, our glorious heritage shall gain,

   And rule our righteous kingdom in the end ;

Though long the day, we shall not be deterred

By any barrier of hope deferred,

   Or any heavy cross that He may send.

" O friend ! my friend ! had I but loved thee more

   When thou wast with me "—this my soul doth say,

Forgetting God's great love did wealth outpour,

   More than a thousand voices could convey ;

The mighty One, Himself, did make thee see

His own illimitable majesty,

   And made thy soul to worship and adore.

It is enough, O God, I am content—

   Thou hast regarded me in lowliness ;

With my weak words Thy mighty voice was blent ;

   And Thou reveal'dst to him true holiness ;

Thou fill'dst the weakness of my poor desire

With strength, that made his heart and soul aspire,

   And Thy dear saving Name with joy confess.

I am content, O God, my cup is filled

   To running over ; lo ! my table spread

With bounties ; and thy grace, like dew distilled,

   Makes my land bloom ; thine oil anoints mine head ;

Thy peaceful streams through my green meadows flow ;

My vines do bud ; my fruit-tree blossoms blow ;

   And heaven's blue dome expandeth overhead.

O Best Belovèd, Thou perfect his soul,

   And purge in fire seven times, as gold refined ;

At last we shall stand up, complete and whole,

   The perfect image of our Father's mind—

All broken laws atoned, all sins made white ;

One mind, one heart—Perfection and Sweet Light,

   Two souls made one, and both in God combined.

The pure and perfect Temple of our Lord,

   Where, as a King enthroned, begins His reign,

His peaceful reign, that knows no slaying sword,

   That comforts sorrows, heals and cleanses pain,

That wipes away all tears from every eye,

That death and hell o'ercomes with victory,

   That soothes the wretched, and restores the slain.

Build Thou a place, Immanuel, our King,

Where Thou canst come and rule in righteousness,

Where men unto Thy Throne can offerings bring,

And where the Priests of God can cleanse and bless:

Holy of Holies, Sanctuary pure,

God set thee up upon foundations sure,

That Israel's woes in thee might find redress.

THE REST OF GOD. Ezekiel xlvii.

" My delight is to be with the children of men."
Proverbs viii. 31.

"A gracious woman shall find glory."—Proverbs xi. 16.

" Behold, the Tabernacle of God is with men, and he will dwell with them, and they shall be his people, and God himself with them shall be their God.

" And God shall wipe away all tears from their eyes : and death shall be no more, nor mourning, nor crying, nor sorrow, shall be any more, for the former things are passed away."
Revelation xxi. 3-4.

" To him that thirsteth I will give of the fountain of the water of life freely.

" He that shall overcome shall possess these things, and I will be his God, and he shall be my son."—Revelation xxi. 6-7.

Thou Rest of God—God-given,

Breath from the Towers of Heaven,

Eternal Sabbath Day ;

Thy Word divine me blesses,

And, 'neath Thy pure caresses,

My dross consumes away.

O winds of God, fresh blowing ;
O streams of God, clear flowing
  From out the holy place,
Cleanse, with thy holy waters,
Lost Israel's sons and daughters,
  That they may see Thy Face.

Flow, like a mighty river,
Eastward and eastward ever,
  Cleansing the great salt sea ;
And trees of God's own planting,
And fruits of God's own granting,
  Shall grow each side of thee.

The leaves shall be for healing ;
The fruits, God's love revealing,
  Shall ripen and expand ;

And, where the water rushes,
New life with vigour gushes,
    And joy on every hand.

The Son of Man, He knoweth
Where'er this torrent floweth,
    All creature-things shall live ;
The healing waters risen,
Now burst as from a prison,
    And full salvation give.

Lo ! thou hast seen it, surely ;
Hold now this truth, so purely,
    That nought can take away ;
And multitudes shall bless thee ;
And kings and queens confess thee—
    The Daughter of the Day.

THE CLOUDY TOWER.

"And thou, O cloudy tower of the flock, of the daughter of
Zion, unto thee shall it come: yea, the first power shall come,
the kingdom to the daughter of Jerusalem."—MICHAES iv. 8.

I cannot hold my little love,

Though on my breast she lies,

Her spirit soars far up above,

And bends from out the skies;

O milk-white pearl, with eyes of dove,

Teach me thy law, and how to prove

Most pure within thine eyes.

I kiss her small white tender hand—

She smiles with pleasant grace;

O Queen of love's enchanted land,

Let me but read thy face;

Some hidden wisdom ·she doth know,

Like wells of light her eyes do glow,

And mystic lore I trace

In every word of her sweet speech,

In quiet and modest brow—

I wonder what the angels teach,

And, are they speaking now ;

O tender, smiling, lovely eyes

That hide the joys of Paradise !

Before that light I bow.

Teach me the song that angels sing,

Teach me how roses blow,

And how the wild bird soars on wing,

And where the spices grow :

Tell me of fishes of the deep,

And why men dream, and how they sleep ;

Thy wisdom I would know.

Where didst thou gather hidden gems

   Of earth, and sea, and air?

Thy brow doth shine with diadems

   Of many a queen most fair;

And Egypt's wonders live in thee;

Assyria builds thy canopy;

   And Babel decks thy hair.

O cloudy Tower of Zion, thou

   With meek and modest mien,

A greater crown adorns thee now,

   Lost Israel's chosen queen.

O let the flowers of summer spring

Beneath her feet, and roses fling,

   And make her pathway green.

O Tower that shin'st—white cloud by day,

　And glowing fire by night—

Leading the people on their way

　To realms of endless light;

O cloudy Tower, we follow thee

From bondage unto liberty;

　Re-build the City bright.

And Jacob shall thy judgments learn,

　And Israel thy laws;

Our Fathers' God, our hearts shall turn

　To join Thy righteous cause;

And love, like a celestial fire,

Shall purify each heart's desire,

　And purge from stains and flaws.

Arise, O Daughter, rise, and tread;

    As iron shall be thy horn,

And brass thy hoofs; our sins lie dead

    Beneath thy righteous scorn;

And many peoples shalt thou beat

In pieces 'neath thy righteous feet,

    Till holiness be born.

O God, and who is like to Thee

    That takest sins away

And castest them beneath the sea?

    Our Lord, to Thee we pray—

In mercy Thou hast set us right,

And called us forth, from death, to light

    Of everlasting day.

Thou hast remembered Abraham,

  Thy chosen friend of old;

Of Moses, Thou the great " I am "—

  Thy Names are manifold,

And in them Israel lives again;

Thou hast rebuilt, in eyes of men,

  Thy temple of pure gold.

A Holy Nation, purified

  And cleansed by searching fire,

Yea, seven times in furnace tried.

  Till hearts to thee aspire;

For thy delights in us are found,

When harps of earth and heaven resound

  With mutual desire.

INTERLUDE.

EARLY LOVE.

How I would like to be with thee alone

    For days and days together,

To talk, and laugh, and sing till days were done,

    In the blue, cloudless weather;

To pluck bright flowers where sucks the honey-bee;

To laugh again, when waters laughed, for glee;

Oh! shall we ever that sweet Eden see?—

    I wonder whether.

Would'st thou not like to be alone with me

    Forever and forever?

We'd know what things had been, and what should be,

    And what should sever;

Sometimes, as birds, we'd build our little nest;

Sometimes, as dolphins, pierce the waves' bright crest;

Each day would bring some new delightful quest,

    We'd weary never.

M

Oh ! are we not indeed as one alone,

Through all our lives together ?

Were not our fates writ on the selfsame stone ?

Our souls, in tether,

Move through all time in mutual ecstacy,

Bound in one fate and yet forever free,—

Sweetheart, this Eden ours shall ever be

Through wind and weather.

Yet, not alone, since saints in Paradise

Are with us ever,

Our prayers with theirs continually do rise,

Death cannot sever ;

Live in us, Lord, and let us live in Thee ;

Thine heart, the haven where we fain would be ;

Drawn by Thy cords of loving kindness, we

Would leave Thee never.

THE THREAD RESUMED.

A SONG OF HOLY DEATH.

I.

" The last enemy that shall be overcome is death.'
" To live is Christ, to die is gain."

Death, holy death, slayer of all things mortal ;

  Death, holy death, be mine that I may live ;

O sweet white death, fling wide for me the portal

  That leads to Paradise—life to me give.

Yea, Christ hath taught me love indeed past knowing,

  His overcoming makes sweet death my friend—

O mystery supreme, beyond all showing—

  For life and death are one, in Him they blend.

O Heavenly Slayer ! Priest of God Eternal !

  What joys are born of death's pure sacrifice ;

O Christ, Thou giver of the life supernal,

  Our life is bought—Thy blood the precious price.

Yea, every human thing by Thee made holy,
   And death itself filled with supremest light,
For Thou didst glorify the manger lowly,
   And made the sepulchre than sun more bright.

My marriage day shall be when death shall take me
   And lead me, all triumphant, to my Spouse;
There shall the songs of victory awake me,
   There shall the conqueror's crown adorn my brows.

O Love of Christ, that crowns e'en death the slayer,
   And makes mine enemy my chosen friend,
I grieve no more for sin, the sad betrayer,
   Since I have seen what shall be at the end.

O victory supreme! supreme surrender!
   O death in life! O life death shall achieve!
Surrounded now by thy celestial splendour,
   Earth fades away—Christ Jèsus, I believe!

A SONG OF HOLY DEATH.

II.

"Death is swallowed up in victory."

Shall it be soon, sweet Lord?

Shall it be soon?

Fade now the stars away,

The sun, the moon,

Fade too; I only see Thy risen light;

I only see Thy face, than stars more bright;

Sinks now my soul in death's entrancing swoon;

My brightest day

Floods with its splendour life's completest noon.

Shall it be swift, dear Friend ?

Shall it be swift ?

The holy moment stay,

Or sword uplift

In angel hands ?—I saw it flash and gleam

In sweet fulfilment of my life's long dream—

I thought to clasp at once the precious gift—

It fades away,

Then flashes bright once more through cloudy rift.

Is the day near, my Spouse ?

Is the day near ?

My holy marriage day ?

Shall it appear

With streaks of light faint glimmering in the east ?

Shall earth awake as to a glad new feast

Where not one eye shall shed a crystal tear,

Nor one hand lay

A wreath of sorrow on my bridal bier ?

Though it be far, dear Lord,

Though it be far,

Yet it shall surely come ;

Bright luminous star

Of promise flash in my blue firmament—

The day is past, the night perchance far spent,

The east is glowing with a crimson bar,—

Star, call me home

Through whirlwind, rushing steeds and fiery car.

"Ask what thou wilt have me to do for thee before I be taken away from thee. And Eliseus said, I beseech thee that in me may be thy double spirit.

" And he answered : thou hast asked a hard thing ; nevertheless, if thou see me when I am taken from thee, thou shalt have what thou hast asked ; but if thou see me not, thou shalt not have it.

" And as they went on walking and talking together, behold a fiery chariot parted them both asunder, and Elias went up by a whirlwind into heaven.

" And Eliseus saw him, and cried, my father, my father, the chariot of Israel and the driver thereof. And he saw him no more: and he took hold of his own garments and rent them in two pieces.

" And he took up the mantle of Elias that fell on him."

IV. KINGS ii. 9-13.

SWAN SONG.

My swan song to thee I sing—
  My last, my best;
  Dying upon thy breast;
Folded my weary wing,
  Folded to rest.

My swan song to heaven I raise,
  Dying with thee;
  Prisoned souls flying free
In upward songs of praise;
  Dying for liberty.

Sweet death with thee to die,
  Ah! who would live?
  What has life now to give?
Here let me lie—
  Jesus, our souls receive.

Triumphant, my last low song

    Sings of sweet death;

    O failing breath!

One last sweet note prolong;

    Hear what Love saith.

" Lo! how our barren waste

    With flowers doth bloom;

    Light fills our narrow tomb—

Oh! sweet foretaste,

    Banished is gloom.

" Hark! how angelic choirs

    Through heaven resound;

    Beasts of earth crouch around;

Our souls aspire

    With upward bound.

" Hell cannot harm us now,

O hearts, rejoice !

Sing with one voice !

Martyr's crown on each brow—

Death is our choice ! "

" Brother, is Christ now risen ? "

" Yea, risen indeed,

Woman's own seed

Burst forth from prison ;

Filled is each human need."

" Brother, is Christ the Spouse ? "

" Yea, my beloved,

He is approved

Chief of our ancient house—

Stone unremoved."

" Is my belovèd thine ? "

" Yea, loved no less ;

Christ Jesus bless,

Make our death so divine,

All shall confess

" Thee King of Judah's line ;

Love's tenderness

Thy wounds redress ;

Thy Bread and Living Wine

All love express."

INTERLUDE.

————◆————

IN MEMORIAM.

I.

Now art thou gone, my friend, now art thou gone—
    Tossing no more on life's tempestuous sea,
    Thy weary bark is moored, thy soul set free,
Thy prison empty, and thy journey done ;
O poor dumb soul, what music hast thou won
    In thy new life ?   What heights of ecstacy
    Hath thy freed spirit gained ?   What joys to be
For thee whose joy-life hath but now begun ?
Here wast thou dark ?—yet there thou shalt be light ;
    Here wast thou dumb ?—there shall thy spirit sing ;
Thy way, confused, perplexed, shall be made right ;
    God will accept thy lowly offering,
Thy stains shall melt away in His pure sight,
    Thy harp resound when He shall touch the string.

II.

Rest, rest in peace!   Oh! blessed be thy sleep,

    May God's own slumbers soothe thy aching breast;

    May heavenly anthems lull thy soul to rest;

May angel-eyes above thee vigil keep—

Soft eyes, serene, that now no longer weep

    As these poor eyes of earth, by grief possessed;

    The kiss of peace on thy calm brows be pressed—

The seal of love that answers from the deep.

Yea, He shall answer, O thou tempest-tossed!

    Thou wandering sheep, strayed from the Shepherd's
        fold—

Did He not seek to save that which was lost?

    And oh! His ways of love are manifold;

He ransomed thee at death's most bitter cost,

    And made thy life precious as Ophir's gold.

III.

Half of my life lies with thee in the grave,

    Half of my hope is buried with thee too,

    Half of my love, for oh ! my heart was true

In dawning youth when its pure faith I gave

In patient trust, hoping its life might save

    From wrecking time ; new springs will bud anew,

    And summer skies spread their expanse of blue—

But will no season yield the past I crave ?

Now thou art dead, the gulf is not so wide,

    Peace reigns in either breast, in either heart,

And where peace dwells, there love must too abide ;

    Our mutual death doth mutual life impart,

Yea, holy death makes me, at last, thy Bride—

    The veil is rent, I see thee as thou art !

PART IV.

—•—•—

THE NEW EARTH.

DEATH IN LIFE.

Away from thee I die,
  Yet death is sweet to me,
For then my soul doth freely fly
  To find its rest in thee.

Away from thee I fade
  As rose torn from its tree,
From whose crushed leaves the perfume made,
  Doth rise in incense free.

So, from our living death,
  A freer life doth spring;
From fainting heart and failing breath,
  Love mounts on airy wing.

ISRAEL.

I.

"Turn again our captivity, O Lord, as the streams in the south."

I walk in the land of death—
  Oh! when will my love awaken?
Come, with life-giving breath,
  To his love, to his long-forsaken?
I walk in the land of gloom—
When will my garden bloom?
When from my barren tomb
  Shall I be taken?

I live in the land of shades—
  Are the mists dispelling?
Will the sun light my gloomy glades
  With his gladness, quelling
Sorrows and bitter tears—
Harvest of stormy years,
Banish the cloudy fears,
  Joy-life compelling?

"*THE PARADISICAL GARDEN OF ROSES.*"

Oh! my love is like a garden of continual delights—

I walk beneath the apple-tree and pluck the fragrant
flowers,

His cooling shade doth shelter me, his fruit my soul
invites

To taste its honeyed, spicy sweets, and rest 'neath
leafy bowers.

Oh! my love is like a garden where the red pomegranates grow,

And grapes put forth their tender bloom and give a
goodly smell,

Where gush the cooling fountains when the soft south
winds do blow,

Where the pleasant blossoms flourish, and the figs
begin to swell.

Oh ! my love is like a garden of cool refreshing shade,
 I sat beneath his shadow and drank his spicèd wine,
His banner—Love—was over me, my fainting soul he
  stayed
With fairest flowers and apples ; oh ! my best beloved
  is mine.

Yea, my love is like the shadow of a goodly apple-tree,
 He calls me his fair Lily, he calls me Sharon's Rose ;
My desire to my belovèd, and his desire to me—
  Among the thorns I am his flower ; he, fairest tree
  that grows.

A BATTLE CALL.

"In the name of our God we will set up our banners."—

PSALM xx. 5.

Wake! for the light grows bright behind the hills,
  Wake! for the star is glimmering in the east,
Wake! for the trump the silence breaks and thrills,
  With four-fold power of angel, man, and bird, and
    beast.

Wake! for the day-spring draweth nigh, more nigh,
  Red grows the dawning of the coming day,
Breaks now the splendour in the eastern sky,
  The conquering race has risen the evil power to slay.

Spread wide thy banners on the east and west,
  Lift high thy standards on the north and south,
Summon thy mighty ones, the hosts of Israel blest,
  Blow, blow the trumpet loud from priestly mouth.

Wake, Israel! wake! lost Israel, to thy tents,
　Thy God hath called thee, with thunders in His
　　voice;
The Bridegroom swiftly rideth, the willing Bride
　　consents—
　Oh! bring her forth rejoicing and hail a people's
　　choice.

Flash, flash ye lightnings, far from eastern skies,
　Reddening the west with keen and glorious flame;
Loud roars the whirlwind, chaff and stubble flies,
　Our idols fall and perish before His wondrous Name.

Come, glorious Spirit, rewarder of the meek;
　Come, chosen people, reclaim the promised land;
Come, wandering exiles, again your country seek;
　Ye multitudes of heaven as numberless as sand.

O Israel's God, restore us, restore Thy chosen race,

    Build Jerusalem, our City, and crown our chosen queen,

Bring the Exiled and the Hidden, each one to his own place,

    And let Thy glory cover us with bright and cloudy sheen.

Let the nations fear before us; let us come beneath Thy Hand;

    With outstretched Arm deliver us, Almighty God, our King;

Give us Abraham's inheritance—bright Canaan's promised land;

Let the captives, now returning, with joy exult and sing.

Jerusalem, our City, we love her very stones,

    Her walls are our salvation, her pearly gates are praise;

And the Holy Land, that sepulchred our fathers'
    sacred bones,
Is the Land where God's own glory those mighty
    bones shall raise.

O God, who chose our father, great Abraham, for
    friend,
Who blest the barren Sarah with holy fruitful seed,
Again Thy mercy blesseth us, again Thy dews descend,
    And all the house of Israel are filled beyond their
    need.

Again the fig-trees flourish, again the deserts bloom ;
    The wasted City 's builded, the Holy Place restored ;
Burst forth in singing, barren one, for lo ! thy fruitful
    womb
    Hath given us Immanuel, our God and Man adored.

Rejoice, rejoice! sing praises with pipes, and harp, and lute,

  With trumpets, and with minstrelsy, ten thousand voices raise;

He shall sit as a refiner, and our earth to gold transmute—

  Our Alpha and Omega, our Ancient One of Days.

LOVE SONG.

White Dove, bright Dove, in rocky clefts abiding,

    Let me see thy countenance, oh ! let me hear thy

      voice ;

White Dove, bright Dove, in rocky places hiding,

    Coo to me, and sing to me, and make my heart

      rejoice.

Bright Dove, white Dove, lonely am I waiting,

    Let me see thy countenance with soft and tender

      eyes ;

Bright Dove, white Dove, other birds are mating,

    Coo to me, and sing to me, before the red rose dies.

Lone love, one love, fades the night in morning,

    Far behind the brown old hills the reddening light

      doth glow ;

Arise, my love, my fair one, make haste to thine
  adorning,
  And come unto the valleys where a thousand roses
    blow.

Fleet love, sweet love, all the earth is springing,
  Green the pastures spreading rich with verdure new ;
Sweet love, fleet love, come with gladness, bringing
  Blessings of the spring-tide like soft distilling dew.

THE NIGHTINGALE TO THE ROSE.

O sweet red Rose!

O Rose with heart of fire!

O sweet red Rose!

O Rose of my desire!

The south wind woos thee, yea, the soft breeze blows;

Open, my Rose,

Before my heart expire!

O sweet red Rose!

My heart doth faint for thee;

Soft leaves, unclose,

Let in thy honey-bee;

On thy fair bosom let thy love repose;

My fragrant Rose,

Open thy heart to me.

O sweet red Rose!

How swift the dark night flies,

How stealthily she goes;

Gray dawn in eastern skies

Is breaking, soon a golden glory glows;

My eastern Rose,

Open thy dove-like eyes.

O sweet red Rose!

Behind the eastern hills

The red sun glows,

His light the morning fills

With gladness, and the dancing river flows,

While the eternal snows

.Blush red with sudden thrills.

O Rose, red Rose!

Rose of my heart's desire,

The south wind blows,

Open thy heart of fire ;

On thy soft bosom let thy love repose,

My own sweet Rose,

Before thy life expire.

Yea, in a single night my red Rose bloomed,

In a single night she oped her heart,

And there, among the petals, is my soul entranced, entombed,

Pierced by the sweetness of Love's dart.

THE SILENT HARP.

I.

Oh ! for the Harp that should again awake
  The sleepers, and the dreamers, and the dead ;
Oh ! for the trump that should this silence break,
  'Till scattered Israel flock to Christ, the Head ;
O voice of thunder, shake their dread repose !
O voice of mercy, heal their ancient woes !
  God of my fathers, let the Word be said.

Your barren land unfruitful is—untilled ;
  Ye wandering exiles, doomed afar to roam,
On alien soil your sacred blood is spilled ;
  Your country desolate of shrine or home ;
Your altar fires have long since ceased to burn ;
O chosen people ! when will ye return ?—
  Cast now on many shores like wind-blown foam.

Might I but sing, once more, the frozen strain,

   'Till memory woke deep echoes in your breasts;

Yea, though the life recalled should come through pain,

   I would sing on as one who never rests

'Till longed for goal be won ; my heart, on fire,

Shall burn 'till Israel's hearts wake with desire

   To hear the Word fulfilling Love's behests.

Might I but light the sacrificial flame ;

   Lost Israel, the nations wait for thee !

Might I but speak the Holy wondrous Name,

   The Truth, the blessed Truth, that makes us free ;

O dear Jerusalem, when I forget

Thine exiles, let my sun forever set,

   Teach me no more thy law of liberty.

Might I but draw the tribes with bands of love,

   And comfort all God's people with my voice,

As tenderly as a full-throated dove

   Sings to its mate, would I their hearts rejoice

With songs of Zion, yea, with songs of praise

And exultation as in olden days ;

   Your fathers' God again makes you His choice.

Yea, as the Bridegroom honoureth the Bride

   With love, and all her beauty doth adorn,

So cometh now thy King, the Crucified,

   To heal thy wounds and wipe away thy scorn ;

Your fathers' curse came down the ages past,

But, oh ! the children shall be blest at last,

   For Israel's glory—risen Christ—was born :

A Light to lighten all the Gentile lands—

   His Bride He shall adorn with Israel's crown,

The Throne of David now forever stands—

   A Child to us is born in Bethlehem town,

A Child that shall forever be our King—

To Him our offerings and our tribute bring;

   O Wonderful!   O Counsellor of renown!

INTERLUDE.

WHEN.

When I am gone,

Read what my hand hath writ ;

O Love ! love on

Over my silent head ;

When summer swallows to the southward flit,

And every drooping flower is witherèd,

When sings no more the drowsy honey-bee,

When the last leaf has fallen from the tree—

Remember, Love, the words that I have said.

· When sunset skies

Grow dark with coming night,

Then turn thine eyes :

Beyond the solemn sea

Another morning waits ; the dawn's gray light

Shall break once more, mine own, for thee and me,—

There waits the love death hath no power to slay,

There breaks the morn of love's perpetual day,

There shall the prisoned soul from chains go free.

When death draws near,
Cover my weary face,—
I shall not fear,
But wait with quiet soul;
Beside the sea be my last resting place,
Where I can hear the far waves beat and roll,—
Watching the sea-birds wheel above thy head,
Thou wilt not dream of me among the dead,
But feel my spirit their white wings control.

When life is past,
Gone like a restless dream;
When at the last
I see the vision fade,
Thy sighs of love shall waft me o'er the stream
Whose swift strong current no man yet hath stayed;
Oh! fill my heart with blessings of deep rest,
Pillow my weary head upon thy breast,
And weep no more when in the grave I'm laid.

THE THREAD RESUMED.

HEBREW PRAYERS.

" O sound thy great cornet as a signal for our freedom: and lift up thy banner to collect our captives, and gather us speedily together from the four corners of the earth, unto our own land. Blessed art thou O Lord! who gatherest together the outcasts of thy people Israel."

"Oh ! restore our judges as aforetime, and our counsellors as at the beginning; and remove from us sorrow and sighing : and speedily, O Lord ! reign thou alone over us in mercy, righteousness and justice.   Blessed art thou, O Lord ! the King who lovest righteousness and justice."

" Oh ! dwell in the midst of Jerusalem, thy city, as thou hast spoken, and speedily establish therein the throne of David, oh ! build it speedily in our days, a structure of everlasting fame. Blessed art thou, O Lord, who buildest Jerusalem."

Joy, like a fire, burns within one, when I bring to mind how I went forth from Egypt. But I can only raise lamentations when I remember how I went forth from Jerusalem."

THE NINTH OF AB.*

Come, mourn with me for one who sits alone
  And solitary as the desert bird,
Come, weep with me, and let our tears atone;
  Shall Zion's songs of joy no more be heard?
To comfort her distress she hath found none,
She suffers for the deeds she hath not done.

The fathers sinned, and now the children weep,
  With tears is choked the music of the voice,
They sowed the wind, and we the whirlwind reap;
  Oh! when shall Israel, as of old, rejoice?
Thou, watching her, dost slumber not nor sleep,
Through the long night Thou dost Thy vigil keep.

---

* A Fast-day of the Jews on which they commemorate their departure from Jerusalem.

Thou hast not pitied us, Thou hast pulled down,

Thou hast fulfillèd all Thy righteous Word ;

Long in the dust hath lain Jerusalem's crown,

Her men and maidens victims of the sword,

Yea desolate sits our city of renown,

For no one buildeth up great David's town.

THE VOICE OF THE SPIRIT.

Peace, He will comfort you in banishment ;

Peace, He will heal the breach, and still your cries ;

Behold, the heavenly Dove to you is sent ;

The Comforter, with subtlest tones, replies ;

Your many wails at length the Heavens have rent,

And choirs above with earthly choirs are blent.

P

THE PEOPLE.

The Name of Sovereign Great be sanctified ;

   Renew our life, O Lord ! revive the dead ;

Prepare Thy people as Thy chosen Bride,

   And place the crown once more on Israel's head ;

Rebuild Jerusalem—let her tears be dried,

She suffereth long—let her be justified.

THE SONG OF DELIVERANCE.

Joy like a fire shall burn

When we go forth,

From East and West return,

From South and North;

From Egypt we went forth in days of old:

Our wondrous triumph shall again be told.

Joy like a fire shall burn

When we return.

Our days of mourning past,

We weep no more;

Our fathers' God, at last

Doth life restore;

With many tears we left Jerusalem,

The wrath of God cast down our diadem.

Joy like a fire shall burn

When we return.

My house He hath rebuilt—

The cloud abides ;

He hath wiped out my guilt,

And none derides ;

He shall restore us to our promised land,

And strengthen us with His Almighty Hand.

Joy like a fire shall burn

When we return.

He blesseth us with corn,

And wine, and oil ;

Exalteth Israel's horn ;

Rewards our toil.

Forth from Jerusalem in grief we went—

Outcasts in many lands, by sorrow sent.

Joy like a fire shall burn

When we return.

By Babel's streams I wept—

Now do I sing ;

Our harps on willows slept—

With joy they ring ;

And tuneful voices chant sweet melodies ;

And lute and lyre awake to songs of praise.

Joy like a fire shall burn

When we return.

With glory, forth I came

From Egypt's night,

Sustained by Thy great Name

And wondrous might ;

When from Jerusalem I did depart,

The sharpened sword was ready for my heart.

Joy like a fire shall burn

When we return.

With days of sabbath rest,

With sign, and feast,

Our coming forth was blest

From great to least ;

But from Jerusalem with mourning fast

I went, and mourn till exile shall be past.

Joy like a fire shall burn

When we return.

There were divisions four,

And goodly tents,

Beside the Red Sea's shore ;

Now battlements

Our tribe withstand ; and warring Ishmaelites ;

A sword of flame Jerusalem's exiles smites.

Joy like a fire shall burn

When we return.

The year for land's release

Was then ordained,

Then rest and fruits' increase

The land obtained;

But when we left Jerusalem land was sold

Forever; and our homes the aliens hold.

Joy like a fire shall burn

When we return.

When Egypt I resigned,—

The Ark was made,

The Mercy-seat designed,

And stones were laid

For a memorial; but when I left

Jerusalem, I was of all bereft.

Joy like a fire shall burn

When we return.

Levites were there, and Priests—

Threescore and ten

Elders; and solemn feasts

Ordained were then;

But when Jerusalem was left behind,

All men oppressed us with one common mind.

Joy like a fire shall burn

When we return.

From Egypt wandering,—

Moses me fed,

And Miriam's voice did ring,

Aaron me led;

But I of Adrian was sore oppressed,

When of Jerusalem no more possessed.

Joy like a fire shall burn

When we return.

When for victorious fight

We did prepare,

We saw the cloudy light,

The Lord was there ;

When from Jerusalem we wandered far,

He guided us no more by cloud or star.

Joy like a fire shall burn

When we return.

The secret place within

The holy veil—

Where cleansed is Israel's sin,

Where prayers prevail—

Ordainèd was when the Lord led me forth

From Egypt ; but Jerusalem met His wrath.

Joy like a fire shall burn

When we return.

With whole burnt offering
And sacrifice
Of fire, we gifts did bring,
And all sweet spice :
When from Jerusalem my face was set,
The precious children sword and whirlwind met.
Joy like a fire shall burn
When we return.

Bonnets of honour, worn
By holy Priests,
Whose glory did adorn
Our ancient feasts ;
When from Jerusalem, uncrowned, we came,
Our glory turned to scorn, honour to shame.
Joy like a fire shall burn
When we return.

The plate of gold, for power,

` On me conferred ;

Dominion was my dower ;

I was preferred

Above the other nations ; now no more

Is seen the crown Jerusalem proudly wore.

Joy like a fire shall burn

When we return.

With prophecy He led

From Egypt's soil,

On heavenly manna fed,

Redeemed from toil

Of cruel tasks, our hosts ; His presence blest

His people, gave them days of sabbath rest.

Joy like a fire shall burn

When we return.

Jerusalem once lost,

With souls unclean,

We wandered, tempest-tossed,

No pathway seen

When from our City we were rudely thrust

To meet the sword or bow us in the dust.

Joy like a fire shall burn

When we return.

I had a glorious song

Of triumph when

I o'ercame Egypt's wrong;

Salvation then

Rang in the trumpets' loud and silvery blast,

When Pharaoh's hosts in the Red Sea were cast.

Joy like a fire shall burn

When we return.

Our children's wailing cries

And piercing groans

Resounded to the skies

When Temple stones

Were scattered, and Jerusalem to the ground

Was razed; her exiled sons to bondage bound.

Joy like a fire shall burn

When we return.

Our candlestick re-light :

Our table spread ;

Our ancient woes requite ;

Let us be fed ;

Again be sanctified by Holy Flame ;

Again be led by power of wondrous Name.

Joy like a fire shall burn

When we return.

When shall we cease to mourn

Our fallen crown?

Immanuel, art Thou born

In Bethlehem town?

Restore the Kingdom, O our Righteous King;

With songs of gladness back Thy people bring.

Joy like a fire shall burn

When we return.

INTERLUDE.

LOVE AND DEATH.

I.

"And thus we must be bound with the woman till we send
her to the grave, and then shall she be a Shadow and a Figure;
and the Virgin shall be our Bride and precious dower."—"The
Three Principles."

JACOB BEHMEN.

The dark eyes of my lover

    Shine in the pale moonlight,

And the curls upon his brow

    Are wet with the dews of night:

And to my heart he presses

With a thousand fond caresses.

    Doth my love his love requite?

Kiss not my lips, fond lover,

    Red lips will soon grow pale,

And though their speech be now

    As the song of the nightingale,

Q

Believe not their consenting,

For death knows no relenting,

   And prayers will not prevail.

Why wilt thou love a shadow,

   A dream born of the night?

Why should I plight a vow

   To break with the morning's light?

Thou canst not seize and bind me;

Thy love will never find me

   In the grave, far out of sight.

LOVE AND DEATH.

II.

I saw the moon behind a fleecy veil ;

I looked and saw my lover's cheek grow pale,—

"Why dost thou sigh ? "

" Alas ! my soul, my heart doth faint and fail

Lest thou should'st die."

I said "Our love, like the moon's silver bow,

Soon to a round and golden fruit will grow ;

Why dost thou weep ? "

" Oh ! lest those eyes, that now so brightly glow,

Should close in sleep ;

" And then, oh ! then would wane my harvest moon,

And then my winter nights come all too soon ;

If thou should'st fade,

Let me, love, sink with thee in death's deep swoon,

Heart-pulses stayed."

I said " Our harvest moon will grow more bright,

Dear heart, for many a long warm summer night,

　　　Why dost thou fear ? "

" Thy little hands, love, are so cold and white,

　　　Thine eyes so clear ;

" Yet lay thy hands upon my burning brow,

And give me kiss for kiss, and vow for vow,

　　　My only love ;

Death shall not steal my bride clasped closely now,

　　　Nor woo my dove."

She laid her head upon his yearning breast,

.And softly sighed her soul away to rest ;

　　　O failing breath !

Love cannot stay thee from immortal quest,

　　　Nor vanquish death.

SONG.

O my lady! O my lady!

In the garden cool and shady;

Roses in thy finger-tips,

Warm red roses on thy lips;

See the honey-bee that sips

Honey from the roses' lips.

O my lady! O my lady!

'Neath the branches cool and shady,

Where the warm red roses blow,

Comes a honey-bee I know,

Sings a love-song sweet and low—

Lovers' songs are sweet I know.

O my lady! O my lady!

When the night grows cool and shady,

When the moon shines round and red,

When the honey-bee hath fled,

Comes the nightingale instead,

Singing when the bee hath fled.

THE THREAD RESUMED.

ISRAEL.

II.

" Mine eyes fail in watching for the fulfilment of thy promise,
saying, when wilt thou comfort me?"

My soul is weary waiting—

Waiting for the day,

Oh! when will come the morning

That I may flee away?

Oh! when will come the morning?

Oh! when will end the night?

Oh! when will rise my glorious sun

In floods of golden light.

My heart is weary weeping,

   Mine eyes are wet with tears,

Oh! when will come the daybreak,

   Dispelling clouds and fears?

Oh! when will come the daybreak,

   My resurrection morn,

When I, as one among the dead,

   To life shall be re-born?

When I among the nations

   Again shall take my place,

My crown restored in glory,

   Recalled mine exiled race;

My crown restored in glory,

   Replanted mine own land,

Rejoicing then in Israel's God

   Who stretched forth His hand

And shook the earth beneath us,

  And shook the heavens above,

And woke all hearts to praise Him

  With tones of mighty love,

Who woke all hearts to praise Him ;

  His chosen race he set

An ensign for the people—

  A shining coronet.

Then shall the songs of Judah

  Again be songs of praise,

His harps no more lamenting

  The long and barren days,

His harps no more lamenting

  By Babylonian streams,

But filled with plenteous vision

  And clear prophetic dreams.

His eyes no longer darkened
  But gifted with strange light,
Beholding cloudy pillar
  By day, and fire by night,
Beholding cloudy pillar,
  Beholding Bethlehem's star,
Guiding him through the desert,
  To promised land afar.

My face toward Jerusalem
  I now again will turn;
The silver trump resounding,
  Joy like a fire shall burn;
The silver trump resounding,
  Shall call the people forth;
Oh! come from East, and come from West,
  And come from South and North.

Again, ye exiled people,

 To your own country come,

Return ye priestly nation,

 Your God hath called you home,

Return ye priestly nation,

 Thou joy of the whole earth,

Break forth again with singing,

 Whom God hath given re-birth.

TWO VOICES.

And dost thou love me?—lo ! thou art repaid,
   For something of me is forever thine ;
   The sun and moon with softer glory shine ;
Mysterious splendour fills the moonlit glade ;
And deeper meaning now hath been conveyed,
   Through Nature's moods, from out thy heart to mine.
   Have we not tasted of the draught divine ?
And seen the wondrous power of God displayed ?
The clouds are brighter now because thine eyes
   Have looked on them with me, the skies more clear,
The flowers are tinged with softer, richer dyes,
   The starry splendours bring thy spirit near,
Within my soul a mirrored heaven lies,
   And at thy coming, sorrows disappear.

THE KING'S DAUGHTER.

" The Word, the Redeemed is such as needs to be washed, and cleansed, and clothed upon.

" In her lives the Imrah, the Word which is distilled and purified."

" The feminine Imrah, or seven times purified words of Elóhah and of Jehovah."

" It is a quickening Word, which comforts in affliction, and is the reward of all who keep Jehovah's precepts."

Mrs. BREWSTER MACPHERSON.

I am beloved of the Prince of the garden of pleasure,

    I am beloved ;

I am his pearl, and his dove, and his heart's hidden

    treasure,

    I am approved ;

To-day he has given his love, oh ! his love without

    measure,

    Which can never be moved.

He has called me " Beloved of my soul," and my heart
        beats, repeating
                " Beloved of my soul,"
And my blood dances swift through my veins in a
        musical beating ;
                The twin currents roll,
Pouring forth their wild love, then again to their centre
        retreating
                Under righteous control.

O king of my life's hidden spring ! O lord of my being !
                Beloved of my heart ;
Our lips breathed one prayer, and our souls, in a
        sudden, agreeing,
                Knit, joining each part
Of the long-severed Word that the prophets beheld in
        their seeing—
                Beloved thou art.

The long-severed name of the Lord we are loving and
    fearing ;
        Our Sabbaths of rest
Do welcome the Son ; the Redeemed hail the Bride-
    groom's appearing—
        His Name ever blest ;
The Word in our hearts spoken now, in soft accents
    endearing,
        With joy is confest.

Yea ! Imrah—the Word, the Redeemed, the Bride of
    the Morning,
        The joy of the earth ;
O Imrah, beloved, whom the world had outcast in its
    scorning,
        Rejoice in thy birth ;
Ten thousands shall bless thee and bring thee thy gems
    of adorning,
        And comfort thy dearth.

R

The gifts of thy lover, with gladness and joy, now
    receiving—
        The jewels and crown ;
Thou hast trusted in Israel's God, and behold, thy
    believing
        Shall make thy renown ;
Thy comforting love shall flow forth with a boundless
    relieving,
        Re-building the Town.

Thou art builded like Eve—from a man, thou art
    builded for blessing,
        And thou shalt be blest ;
Thy vineyard shall yield the best grapes with our
    pruning and dressing,
        Yea, thy vine shall be dressed,
And our Dove shall return to her land and receive our
    caressing,
        And build her soft nest.

Thou comest with wine and with joy, O Jerusalem's
daughter—
Thou comest with love,
And thy wine, like the wine of the Master that turnèd
from water,
Brings joy from above,
For Wisdom, thy Mother, instructed her daughter and
taught her;
Thou art Israel's Dove!

Thou comest with love and the Olive—the Branch thou
art bearing—
The promise of peace;
And all the wild tumults of waters art braving and
sharing
To bring our release;
And thy voice, in sweet accents of love, now to us is
declaring
That tumults shall cease.

O Israel's Dove, hie thee swift, for our lone hearts are
    waiting
        And calling for thee ;
Art thou near, O my Dove ?   Are the waters of strife
    now abating
        O'er the wide rolling sea ?
Or are the fierce waves of destruction their cruelty
    sating
        On the bond and the free ?

O Dove of our peace, hie thee swift, and thy love shall
    restore us—
        Thou art Israel's dower ;
Thy banner of love soon in triumph shall flutter before
    us—
        The symbol of power ;
And a voice from the sky shall descend like a vast
    blessing o'er us—
        Behold here thy tower.

Yea, tower of our strength, rocky fortress, a thousand
defending
By power of the Word;
O accents where justice and love in accord now are
blending,
Yet sharper than sword;
Thou fire that consumest our sins, yet, in mercy
descending,
Revealest the Lord.

Lo! our desert doth bloom, and our wells of fresh
water, upspringing,
Shall comfort and heal;
Our mourning shall turn into joy, and our sadness to
singing,
For thou dost reveal
The deep hidden treasures of Wisdom, to light thou
art bringing
What time did conceal.

Oh! turn us again Father-God, yea, our hearts are
      returning,
            Our faces are set;
Jerusalem, our Mother, for thee all thy children are
      yearning;
            Shall Judah forget?
Lo! the altar fires deep in our souls are rekindled
      and burning,
            Our eyes still are wet.

Oh! bring us again to our land, let the loud trumpet
      calling,
            Gather in from afar;
The temples of Babel are shattered, the stones now
      are falling—
            Follow Bethlehem's star,
It has risen in splendour; comes now, with a beauty
      appalling,
            The chariot car.

PRAYER.

" Prayer is Israel's only weapon, a weapon inherited from its fathers, a weapon tried in a thousand battles."—THE TALMUD.

" Watch and pray lest ye enter into temptation."

If temptation bar thy way,

Ceaseless watch and ceaseless-pray—

Evil powers, resisted, flee,

Prayer shall give thee victory.

If there lurketh secret sin,

Hidden deep the heart within—

Ceaseless watch and ceaseless pray,

Prayer the evil power shall slay.

If the soul, o'erwhelmed with pain,

Feeleth deadly foes regain,

For a moment, rule and power—

Prayer shall rescue in that hour.

Watch and pray, thy God shall hear—

" Trouble not your hearts ·with fear ";

Brother, Rescuer, and Friend,

Be Thou with us to the end.

INTERLUDE.

"Love your wife like yourself, honour her more than yourself: whosoever lives unmarried, lives without joy, without comfort, without blessing. * * * He who sees his wife die before him, has, as it were, been present at the destruction of the sanctuary itself; around him the world grows dark. * * * It is woman alone through whom God's blessings are vouchsafed to a house. She teaches the children, speeds the husband to the place of worship and instruction, welcomes him when he returns, keeps the house godly and pure, and God's blessings rest upon all these things."—THE TALMUD.

LOVE AND DEATH.

III.

" Why are thine eyes so bright to-night ? "

" Sweetheart, because I love thee so."

" Why is thy cheek so wan and white—

Thy little hands like flakes of snow ?

Thou can'st not hide that falling tear,

Tell me, my love, what dost thou fear ? "

" Lest I must leave thee, dear, and go."

" Thou shalt not go my love, my bride,

Death shall not tear thee from my heart,

The cruel grave shall never hide

Thy dear white form—where'er thou art

There will thy faithful lover be,

Then take me to the grave with thee,—

Death shall not hold us long apart."

" Nay, loved one, live—the sun will shine,

    The birds will sing, the flowers will bloom,

And other eyes will glow like mine

    When I am hidden in the tomb ;

Thou can'st not stay my fleeting breath ;

Thou can'st not rescue me from death ;

    Why would'st thou share my silent doom ?

" Live on, love on, when I am dead,

    The rose must fade that bloomed to-day ;

When others bloom above my head,

    Drink in their fragrance while ye may,

And scatter their bright crimson leaves

Above the heart that no more grieves

    At any word thy lips can say.

" Live on, love on a little while,

Perchance the echoes of my song

Thy lonely heart will then beguile ;

Life cannot vex thee very long,

And thou again shalt see my face,

And come to my abiding place,—

Though death be sure, yet love is strong.

" Yea, thou again shalt bring me rest,

I shall but sleep and dream of thee,

And long to lie upon thy breast,—

The grave were not too cold for me

If thou wert sleeping by my side ;

Methinks with thee I might abide

In blessèd dreams eternally.

" I shall not wish again to wake,

  Nor any further joy to know ;

The everlasting day may break,

  The seasons come, the seasons go,

The long slow ages onward creep,

If heart to heart we, dreaming, sleep ;

  Let time like a smooth river flow.

" Life lasteth but a little hour,

  And then the soul must flee away,

Nor any word of love hath power

  To bid the fleeting spirit stay,—

It bursts from shell with airy wings,

And in exultant freedom sings,

  Leaving its prison-house of clay.

" And tenderest beauty turns to dust,

 E'en as the rose must droop and fade ;

As worn-out tools corrupt with rust,

 So years destroy the youth they made,—

Yea, the inevitable years

Cancel our smiles and dry our tears—

 Nor life, nor death, can make afraid."

IN MEMORIAM.

MARIE.

And do men call thee dead thou blighted flower?

   And do men call thee dead because blind Love

Hath slain thee with his tumults in an hour?—

   One fatal hour; thy soul still waits above

For consummation of thy vision bright,

   For consummation of thy vision blest,

That soon shall turn earth's darkness into light,

   And bring our labouring days to sabbath rest.

Thy prisoned heart on earth no longer beats;

   Thy soul, in anguish, bursts its fragile shell,

But lo! a seraph's voice thy song repeats

   As thou art borne afar where angels dwell.

Soon shalt thou walk Jerusalem's golden streets—'

   Ere our sad hearts have ceased to weep "farewell."

SONG.

This love that surgeth in my breast,

That surgeth like a sea,

This love that will not give me rest,

That panteth to be free,—

Calm thou its tides, O vision blest,

And bid it come to thee !

This love that burneth in my heart,

That burneth like a flame,

Of sacrificial fires a part,

Ascending whence it came,—

Oh ! let it guide me where thou art,

Revealer of the Name.

This love that fluttereth in my soul,

   That trembleth like a bird,—

Do thou its fiery breath control,

   But let its voice be heard

Clear when the seven thunders roll,

   Revealer of the Word.

LOVE AND DEATH.

IV.

Live, live with me to see the white clouds float
　　Across the azure sky,·to watch the sea,
To hear the music from the skylark's throat,
　　To know the joy of life—the ecstacy;
Live, live with me through long warm summer days,
And hear the woodlands thrill with songs of praise,
　　And watch the plover piping o'er the lea.

The earth is fair, beloved, the spring is sweet,
　　The wild flowers bloom within the bosky dell,
The grass grows green beneath our gladsome feet,
　　And notes of many a bird, that we love well,
Come ringing through the shadows of green boughs;
Ah! twine spring's fragrant blossoms on my brows,
　　And let our eyes our heart's great rapture tell.

The spring is sweet, beloved, the earth is fair,

  And tender are the blossoms of the vine,

Wild music floats on waves of golden air,

  And floods the earth with melody divine,

And yet, O sweetest heart, if thou should'st die,

Silent would grow my life, and dark my sky;

  Open thy grave and lay my heart with thine.

Live, live with me, beloved, or let me die;

  When thy dear eyes do close, shut out my sight,

I will not see the azure of the sky,

  But only deepest gloom and dark midnight,—

The earth will be my tomb when thou art dead,

Then lay my heart on thine, pillow my head

  Upon thy breast, and let our souls take flight.

THE THREAD RESUMED.

ISRAEL.

III.

O Israel! with my latest breath,
  And with my dying hand,
I'll sing of thee and write thy praise,
  And long for thee, my land,
For thy quiet streams, deep flowing,
For thy hills where grapes are growing,
  For thy trees whose fruits expand.

Jerusalem, my dying eyes
  Toward thy hills shall turn,
My last deep sigh shall breathe thy name,
  My heart's last throb shall burn
With love of thee, poor city
O'er which Christ's heart in pity
  Like a mother's heart did yearn.

O holy land! O sacred soil!

I would my feet might tread

Where Abraham and Sarah dwelt,

Whither the tribes were led;

Oh! where their bones are lying,

There would I fain be dying,

There rest with mine own dead.

THE CHARIOT OF ISRAEL.

My life doth grow more lovely at its close,

And green the pastures for my weary feet,

The chariot is near, yet now more sweet

Than ever blooms each red-lipped fragrant rose;

The peace of God in music round me flows;

Nature's full hands, with bounteous joys replete,

Bring corn and wine and oil, her songs repeat

The praise of sabbath rest and Heaven's repose;

We have not laboured long, yet rest is near—

Our exile ended, God doth call us home,

Through the bright clouds the chariot-wheels appear,

The voice, as of a trumpet, bids us come;

Beyond the whirlwind shines the amber clear,

The fiery temple, and the azure dome.

THE IMMUTABLE.

Talk to the fire and bid it cease from burning,

Talk to the wind and bid it cease to blow,

Talk to my heart and bid it cease from yearning,

Talk to the waves and make them cease to flow,—

As fruitless words 'gainst water, wind, and fire,

So are your words against my heart's desire!

The fire aspireth upward in its burning,

And like the Spirit's breath the wind doth blow,

And God will cleanse my heart through its deep
yearning,

His waves of judgment round about me flow,

He purgeth me by water, wind, and fire,

His Word shall give me all my heart's desire.

THE TRUE FRIEND.

Who is my friend ?—not he who bids me rest
  Because the rocky steep is hard to climb,
Whose summer roses, in my pale hands pressed,
  Have withered in the winds of autumn time,
But he whose voice arouses me from sleep,
And bids me brave the rocks and chasms deep,
  To breathe the air on lonely heights sublime.

My Master calls, and I must haste away,
  He maketh me to rest in my sore need,
Again through lonely vigils bids me pray.
  Or follow where his blessèd footsteps lead ;
The thorns press deep, sharp are the flinty stones,
The quivering flesh in anguish sobs and groans,
  The tears fall fast, the weary feet do bleed ;

And yet Thy yoke is easy, O my Lord !
  Thy rest secure and sweet, Thy burden light,
The awful smitings of Thy two-edged sword
  Have roused my slumbering soul to seek the right ;
In righteousness our only joy is found,
With praise to God let heights and deeps resound,—
  The joys of heaven the woes of earth requite.

THE EVENING OF THE SABBATH.

HEBREW PRAYERS.

" Come, my beloved, to meet the bride ; the presence of the Sabbath let us receive."

" O come let us go to meet the Sabbath, for it is the fountain of blessing ; in the beginning, of old it was appointed ; though last in act yet it was first in thought."

" Sanctuary of a King, O royal city, arise Jerusalem ! come forth from thy subversion ; too long didst thou abide in the vale of tears ; He *(thy God)* will surely compassionate thee."

" Shake off the dust, O my people ! Arise ! array thyself in glorious apparel, for through the son of Jesse the Bethlehemite shall redemption draw nigh to thy soul."

" Arouse ! arouse ! thy light is come, arise and shine forth ! Awake ! awake ! chaunt a hymn ! for the glory of the Lord is revealed upon thee."

" Be not ashamed, *O Jerusalem !* neither be thou confounded. Why art thou dejected ? why disquieted ? In thee shall the poor of my nation again find a refuge, when the city shall be built in her own ruins."

" Then those who spoiled thee shall become a spoil, and those who would fain have devoured thee shall be removed away ; thy God will rejoice in thee as a bridegroom rejoices with his bride."

" To the right and to the left shalt thou extend ; and the eternal God thou wilt revere, and we, by means of a man, a descendant of Parez, will rejoice and be glad."

" Then come in peace, crown of thy husband ; come with joy and exultation amidst a faithful and beloved nation. O come ! come, O bride ! "

Our glorious rest shall be sanctified,

  Our labour ended from eve to eve ;

Come, belovèd, to meet the Bride,

  The Sabbath presence let us receive.

Come, belovèd, go forth to meet

  The Sabbath—the fountain of blessing and rest,

Labour is ended, let joy complete

  With sevenfold praises the Name most blest.

Come, belovèd, to meet the Bride ;

  Our labour is ended from eve to eve,

Our glorious rest shall be sanctified,

  The Sabbath presence let us receive.

O royal City ! arise ! come forth !

  Long hast thou dwelt in the vale of tears,—

Now will He pity, who once was wroth,

  Tenderly banish thy griefs and fears.

Come, belovèd, the Bride to meet,—
  Fountain of blessing and garden of rest,
Roses bloom 'neath her happy feet,
  Lilies sleep on her virgin breast.

Come, from the darkness of death arise,
  Shine again, for thy light is come,
Day of sadness forever dies,
  Words of song call thy spirit home.

Let us go forth to meet the Bride,—
  Fountain of blessing and garden of bloom,
The Eternal His people hath sanctified,
  Raised them up from the barren tomb.

With beautiful garments of light adorn
  Yourselves, my people, the Bride is near;
In clouds of glory the Sabbath morn
  Shall break, the Bridegroom with joy appear.

T

Come, belovèd, the Bride to meet,—
  Garden of roses, and fountain of rest,
With words of song make her welcome sweet ;
  With fine white linen let saints be dressed.

O royal City be not cast down,
  Neither confounded, nor yet ashamed,
The poor of my people beneath thy crown
  Shall shelter, the outcasts shall be reclaimed.

Come, belovèd, to meet the Bride ;
  Blessings of rest and of joy complete
Flow from the fountain—the sanctified,
  Bitter waters by streams made sweet.

The spoilers soon shall become the spoil,
  Those who distressed thee removed away ;
Rejoice in labour,—then rest from toil,
  In holy peace keep thy Sabbath day.

Come, belovèd, the Bride to meet ;

   As the Bridegroom glad, doth thy God rejoice ;

Honour, and glory, and praises sweet,

   Lift, O my people, with trumpet voice.

The Son of Jesse the Bethlehemite

   Hath brought redemption—it draweth nigh ;

O come, belovèd, let us invite

   The Sabbath blessing that waits on high.

Come in peace, yea, in joy and mirth,

   The crown of thy husband, the sanctified ;

The faithful, the chosen redeemed from dearth

   Cry—enter, oh ! enter, a Bride ! a Bride !

Let us go forth, for the way is sweet,

   Garden of spices and fountain of rest ;

Roses bloom 'neath thy happy feet,

   Lilies sleep on thy virgin breast.

THE ETERNAL REFUGE.

"The Eternal God is thy refuge and underneath are the everlasting arms."—DEUTERONOMY xxxiii. 27.

May He watch over thee,
May His wings cover thee,
  Soothe thee to rest,
While thou art sleeping free
He will watch keeping be,
  Over thy nest.

If woe should thee betide,
Then may'st thou with Him hide—
  Safe and secure;
When foes shall thee deride,
Under His wings abide,
  With Him endure.

He shall defend thee still,

By power of righteous will

  Make thy way plain,

He shall thy prayers fulfil,

Guard all thy life, until

  Joy end thy pain.

His mercy shall not cease.

Blessings of love increase—

  Corn, wine and oil.

Rest, weary heart, in peace,

Soon shall He bring release,

  Rest from thy toil.

Under His brooding wing,

There let thy spirit sing

  Praises of love ;

Angels to thee shall bring
Songs sweet, and cherubs fling
 Flowers from above.

Oh ! let thy spirit rest,
Sleep on the holy breast—
 He bids thee sleep ;
Ended thy weary quest,
See now, God's visions blest,
 Eyes that did weep.

Open thine inner eyes,
Joy reigns within the skies,
 Dost thou not see ?
Darkness before him flies,
Earth now to heaven replies
 Israel is free !

Prophet, oh! weep no more,
In joy thy God adore,—
  His face doth shine,
On thee His blessings pour,
Naught that thou can'st implore
  But shalt be thine.

With love thy life is crowned,
Loud let His praise resound.
  Let tongue confess,
Blessings of joy abound;
Thou yet shalt be renowned,
  All hearts shall bless;

Bless thee, for thou did'st find
Help for the weak and blind;
  Thy work shall stand;

Teach men thy law so kind,
Till all of willing mind
Uphold thy hand.

God shall establish thee,
Set thine own people free,
Make thee His own;
O blessèd company,
Soon shalt thou gathered be,
Under the Throne.

THE SPACES OF SWEET GARDENS.

" The female searches sea and land for gratifications to the male genius, who, in return, clothes her in gems and gold, and feeds her with the food of Eden, hence all her beauty beams; she creates, at her will, a little moony night and silence with spaces of sweet gardens and a tent of elegant beauty closed in by a sandy desert and a night of stars shining and a little tender moon and hovering angels on the wing."—WILLIAM BLAKE.

Come, belovèd, where the roses

   Bloom and bloom throughout the night,

Where the soul in sleep reposes

   'Till the early dawning light,—

Dim old garden of sweet spaces,

Shady nooks and hallowed places,

   Tender moon and blossoms white.

Come, belovèd, where the spices

   Shed and spread their odours rare,

Where the crimson rose entices

   Nightingale to thrill the air;

Wide the desert gleams behind us,

Here secure, no foe can find us,

   No wild creature spring from lair.

Far above the clouds are shining,

   And the tender crescent moon

On the fleecy clouds reclining

   Makes the night as clear as noon,

And the trees, above us bending,

Shed their pure white blossoms, sending

   Petal showers like snow in June.

Boughs and branches, interlacing,

   Form a green tent overhead,

And the darkness now is tracing

   Curtains where the shadows spread,

While angelic wings above us

Silently caress and love us,

   While our souls in sleep are fed.

THE LOVE TREE.

" Of two spiritual martyrdoms wherewith God cleanseth the soul that He unites with Himself."

" They cried unto the Lord in their trouble, and He delivered them out of their distresses."—PSALMS.

" Now you shall know that God uses two ways for cleansing the souls which he would perfect and enlighten to unite them closely to Himself.

" The first is with the bitter waters of affliction, anguish, distress, and inward torments.

" The second is with the burning fire of an inflamed love, a love impatient and hungry.

" Sometimes He makes use of both in those souls which He would fill with perfection. Sometimes He puts them into the strong steeping of tribulation and inward and outward bitterness ; scorching them with the fire of rigorous temptation ; sometimes He puts them into the crucible of anxious and distrustful love, making them fast there with a mighty force.

" O that thou wouldest understand the great good of tribulation."

MOLINOS.

My love it grew and grew,

But whether a rank strong weed,

Or a giant fungus growth,

Or a stately goodly tree,

Alas! I never knew;

To kill it, my heart was loth,

Nor could its death decree;

Nor smother its fatal seed,

Until the thunder and lightning came,

And shattered the tree with bolt and flame.

And then a cross was made

From the trunk of the stricken tree,

And on it hung a pale wan shade,

And the mount was Calvary;

My cries are stilled, I weep no more,

But my Saviour God I do adore,

Who brought me victory.

THE LILY FLOWER.

"I will plant my Lily-Branch in my Garden of Roses, which brings me forth fruit, after which my soul craves, of which my sick Adam shall eat, that he may be strong and may go into Paradise."

JACOB BEHMEN.

O my pallid lily!

Lily of the valley—

O my fragile lily!

Wan and white and fair,

Let no winds blow chilly,

O'er my tender lily,

But let south winds dally

With her soft bright hair.

Lily, fair and tender,
  Lean upon my breast,
Lily, lithe and slender,
  Sleep, and dream, and rest.
Oh! may Heaven send her
Dews of health, and lend her
  Visions of the blest.

Doth my lily languish,
  Fading like the rose,—
Then my heart, in anguish,
  Throbs 'till south wind blows,
Yea, my heart it yearneth,
'Till the spring returneth,
  Melting winter's snows.

Lily, pallid lily,

 Mid the green leaves hiding,

When the airs grow stilly,

 I, with thee abiding,

Watch the starry night,

And the moonbeams white,

 Through the tree-tops gliding.

O my pale white lily!

 Like a moonbeam flower,

In the moonlight stilly,

 Bloom for me an hour;

And thy rippling laughter

I shall hear hereafter,

 Like a moonbeam shower.

O my lily blossom !

  Flower of strange delight,

Live within my bosom

  Hidden out of sight :

Be my heart thy bower,

O my sacred flower !

And thy tent of beauty,

  Be the silent night.

"LIVING OR DYING, WE ARE THE LORD'S."

All comes from Thee, my Lord, all comes from Thee,
   Whether it be the sunshine or the rain,
   Whether it be heart-joy or weary pain,
The storm-crowned mountain or the rolling sea;
Thou givest me defeat or victory,
   Thou woundest me and Thou dost heal again,
   I live by Thee, and I by Thee am slain,
Thou bindest me with cords, Thou settest free;
If I with Thee upon the altar die,
   Or if I wander lone on rocky steeps,
Or if on incense-laden air I fly,—
   Thy hand in righteousness my spirit keeps,
   Thou bear'st me up through the great watery deeps;
Yea, though Thou slay me, I on Thee rely.

O STARRY SKIES.

O starry skies, wherein my loved one dwells,

    O skies serene !   O dome of heavenly blue !

    Lift up my heart in silence unto you,

Ye glorious lights whose harmony foretels

The rapture that shall be ; whose joy compels

    The prisoned soul to break its chains anew,

    And with bright wings pierce the dark storm-clouds

        through

Above the tolling of earth's solemn knells.

Yea, let me rise to those celestial heights

    Where I may drink of pure and living streams ;

A melody supreme my soul invites,

    And in its music fades all earthly dreams ;

My sun has risen, and earth's lesser lights

    Pale in the splendour of his glorious beams.

THE HOLY DAY.

Draws nearer and more near the holy day

    When our two souls shall be as one in Him,—

    Earth fades away, the starry host grows dim.

O fiery chariot wheels, make no delay,

Appear, 'mid amber clouds, to bear away

    Our souls through aisles of kneeling cherubim,

    Through holy choirs of chanting seraphim,

While trumpets sound, 'mid harps the harpers play,

Harmonic waves and chords of golden light,

    Entrancing visions fade and disappear,

The throne of splendour gleams within our sight—

    Our spirits pale with love, and throb with fear ;

Upon the throne sits One in raiment white

    Whose eyes shine deeper than the heavens clear.

THE BRIDE'S DESIRE.

O Jesus, make me like to Thee,
  Pour in Thy righteousness,
I hunger, and I thirst to see
  Thy living tenderness ;
The multitudes I fain would feed
With Thy pure love—the bread indeed.

O Jesus, make me like to Thee,
  Thou bruised and broken one !
That waiting eyes may in me see
  Thy will fulfilled and done ;
Pour in, sweet Lord, Thy righteousness,
And give me power to save and bless.

O Jesus, clothe me with Thy love,
  Pure linen fine and white,
Pour down Thy graces from above,

Let gentleness invite

The worn and weary hearts to rest,

As children sleep on mother's breast.

Jesus, my Love, my Lord, my Spouse,

Oh ! make me worthy Thee ;

My sterile soul awake, arouse,

And set my spirit free ;

Thy wondrous eyes I long to meet,

Thy voice to hear in accents sweet.

O Lamb of God ! Incarnate Word !

Where the full Godhead dwells,

My soul's Beloved, my Life, my Lord,

Whose Word my soul compels,

Come, re-create Thyself in me,

Proclaim the law of liberty.

EPITHALAMIUM.

Oh! in thine arms to lie

While the night floateth by,

　The dark majestic night;

To watch the stars grow pale,

When dawn doth night assail

　With pinions vast and bright.

Oh! in thine arms to sleep,

While stars do vigil keep,

　On thy true heart to rest,

'Till from the golden morn

Another day is born,

　In radiant splendour drest.

Pale moon and golden sun,

My bride-day hath begun,

My holy marriage morn;

Sun, moon, and starry skies

Sing, while glad earth replies,—

True Love, sweet Love is born.

O dark blue dome of heaven,

O stars whose lights are seven,

Night melts to golden day,

And life eternal streams

From warm and living beams

'Till death consumes away.

Our souls triumphant stand,

Lords of the sea and land,

Nor time nor space debars,

We reach celestial heights.

In our swift eagle flights,

  Beyond sun, moon, and stars.

The tree of Paradise,

Lost to our parents' eyes,

  The living holy tree

With twelve celestial fruits,

With healing leaves and roots,

  Is ours eternally.

The sword of Cherubim

Before our love grows dim,

  And at our wondrous word

The beasts of earth uprise,

With glad benignant eyes,

  To see man as their lord.

The rapture of our peace

Brings souls in torment ease,

   Our holy love doth flow

To all created things,

And joy eternal brings

   To souls above, below.

The great and holy One

Doth know, His Will is done,

   And His inspiring breath

Fills now, with new-made life,

The risen man and wife

   Born from the womb of death.

Yea, breathe upon us, Lord,

Created by Thy word,

   Pure Bride and holy Spouse,

Breathe now upon Thy slain;

Dear Lord, we live again,

   Rebuild our ancient house.

O great foundation stone,

Built by Thy love alone

   Our house shall ever be,

This shall forever stand,

For God's own righteous hand

   Hath set His people free.

Christ Jesus, righteous King,

Our crowns to Thee we fling,

   Hail, hail, O holy Lord !

Henceforth all wars shall cease,

King of our righteous peace,

   Immanuel—the Word.

Thou art our righteousness,

Saviour, Thy Name we bless,

Thou art our living King,

Ever and evermore

Thee shall our souls adore,

And rapturous praises sing.

Praise with the harp and voice,

Peoples and tribes rejoice,

Nations, throughout the earth,

Join with the heavenly choir,

Let earth to heaven aspire,

Praising a nation's birth.

Ring, ring, O marriage bells!

'Till all your music tells

What triumph love hath won,

Ring, ring, and never cease
'Till the earth cries at peace,
  " This holy love hath done."

Ring out o'er land and sea
Of the glad victory,
  Let your wild music float,
'Till earth's remotest isles
Grow green beneath our smiles
  And learn our glad sweet note.

INTERLUDE.

SONG.

Thine anguish for my sin

   Pierced my heart like the slayer's knife,

And the new life did begin ;

   From the woe, and the waste, and the strife,

And from thy holy pain,—

My soul was born again,

   Eternal Bride and Wife.

SONG.

As silver moonlight on the sea,

   As crystal fountains flowing forth,

So is thy pure white love to me.

   As " chaste as ice " in frozen north,

Like the clear beam of moon or star,

It shines upon me from afar.

As snow on the eternal hills

   Where cold clear airs blow fresh and keen,

As bubbling founts and rushing rills,

   And grots where lily-blooms are seen,—

So is thy love's unchanging light

Than flowers more fair, than snows more white.

As dews reflect the shining morn

  On leaf and blade and blossoming tree,

So doth thy purity adorn

  My risen soul, my spirit free,

So doth thy bride with jewels shine,

Whose depths reveal thy love divine.

THE THREAD RESUMED.

THE SILENT HARP.

II.

O silent harp, awake ! lost Israel's joy,

  Awake ! awake ! with glad triumphant song,

To tune thy strings shall be my dear employ,

  'Till thy sweet melodies ring loud and long,

'Till Israel camps on her forsaken hills,

And Judah's praise the prophet's word fulfils.

O silent harp, neglected were thy strings,

  Broken thy music, dumb thy sweet refrain,

And now on alien shores one lone voice sings

  Of Israel's exile, and of Judah's pain,

But tens of thousands yet shall sing that note

In unison as from a single throat.

Ye scattered sheep, ye lost and wandering tribes,

The Shepherd calls you back unto one fold,

Judah no more shall fear the scorns and gibes

Of alien people, envious of his gold,—

Refined seven times in furnace fire,

His soul shall upward mount with pure desire.

On Joseph rests the everlasting trust,

The birthright is on him, though counted dead;

The treasure, incorrupt of moth or rust,

Shall feed the multitudes; and Christ, the Head,

Through the sweet bounty of His chosen Bride,

Shall see His people fed and satisfied.

Almighty Father, glorious, wondrous King,

I am Thy daughter—be it unto me

According to Thy Will; with joy I sing

A nation's birth—a risen people free ;

In David's harp I bid the music wake,

And all its thousand strings with rapture shake.

It is enough, for Joseph is alive,—

All the long years of woe and lonely pain

Forgotten are—his corn doth make us thrive;

The nations, saved by Joseph's garnered grain,

Atone for all the exile and the loss ;

God's glory streams triumphant from the Cross.

If Israel cast away the Gentiles brought,

What shall the glory of our gathering be ?

When God shall find, at last, the love He sought,

When willing hearts yield tribute glad and free,

When all the tribes in Judah's King rejoice,—

Shall not all nations praise Him with one voice ?

Joseph and Judah! lo! the sticks were twain,

But now are one—Beauty and loving Bands;

Our hearts are turned to Thee, O Lord, again!

With sacrifices filled are priestly hands:

Build us again, O Lord, by Thy pure Word,

Redeem us from the fire and blood-red sword.

The silver now is Thine, the gold is Thine,

The cattle, too, upon a thousand hills;

And Thou hast sanctified our bread and wine;

Thy love within our hearts Thy law fulfils,

We tune our harps, and Thy sweet Name we praise,

Which giveth honour, wealth, and length of days.

INTERLUDE.

INTERLUDE.

LOVE AND DEATH.

V.

With three white roses on her breast,

    And a white rose in her hair,

I thought my maid the loveliest,

    I thought my love most fair,

She seemed, in her white raiment drest,

    A rose beyond compare.

With three white lilies in her hands,

    And lilies on her head,

My maiden wife before me stands,

    And smiles as smile the dead ;

An hour-glass drops its golden sands

    'Till one full hour has sped.

O maiden wife !   O dear lost love !

Pale rose, and lily white,

O my full-throated nestling dove,

My morn, my noon, my night,—

Take my sad soul to thine above,

And teach me heaven's delight.

FOREVER.

Forever !—who can say ?   And yet I know
    That while I live I never shall forget,
    Nor thou in all the long years coming yet ;
Through summer's heat, through winter's frost and
        snow,
Through tempests wild and softest airs that blow,
    Through smiling lips and eyes with tear-drops wet,—
    Shall shine one hour, the hour our spirits met,
For heaven above forecasts the life below.
Forever !—yes ; while this immortal soul
    Knows conscious life, one thought must ever be
Its central fiery breath, must life control,
    And to that life yield strength and impulse free ;
A dual power doth now between us roll—
    Essential joy and new-found liberty.

THE THREAD RESUMED.

THE NEW MARY.

This is the place and this the shrine
  Where my sweet Mary prays for me,
My prayers are hers as hers are mine,
  Hope, faith, desire, in each agree,
We honour our dear Spouse and Lord,
Jesus—sweet Name, with joy adored!

Our willing hearts shall be His Throne,
  Our blended souls His Temple white,
There shall He reign as King alone,
  And fill our darkness with His light,
And through our veins, like fire, shall run
The righteousness of God the Son.

Pour in, sweet Lord, thy golden fire,

'Till every sense be purified,

Let hope and faith and love conspire

To cleanse the body of the Bride,—

With gold her clothing shall be wrought,

When she shall to her King be brought.

As Bride upon the Bridegroom waits,

And yields, with love, to do his will,

So our sweet Spouse in us creates

Desire that shall His Word fulfil ;

And springs and founts of tenderness

Shall all the land with gladness bless.

A VISION OF JUDGMENT.

"And now, little children, abide in him ; that when he shall
appear, we may have confidence, and not be ashamed before him
at his coming."—I. JOHN ii. 28.

I.

Not in Thy wrath, O Lord ! did'st Thou appear,

But in Thy beauty, seen of every eye,

And every tongue confessed Thee passing by,

And every heart saw its beloved draw near—

And, in the knowing, quaked with inward fear,

And longed to meet Thy gaze and longed to fly ;

I mourned, as others mourned, scarce knowing why,

'Till soul's beloved called me by name most dear,—

Then suddenly the woe of banishment

My heart subdued, and love's most righteous scorn,

Like piercing arrows, through my soul was sent,

Until I wept and wailed like one forlorn ;

And myriad anguish cries with mine were blent

When love at last from stony hearts was torn.

II.

Ah! shall I see my soul's dear Spouse and King,

Only to feel severed from my true Lord?

I know love holds the separating sword;

The conqueror aside in scorn must fling

The rebel hosts, who their forced tribute bring.

He seeketh out the doers of His Word,—

The flock who followed when His voice was heard,

And waited not for trumpet blast to ring.

Seeing Thy beauty then, alas! too late,

In darkness and in gloom our souls, outcast,

Deprived of their Adored, must weep and wait

Until the judgment cloud be overpast,—

Then He, perchance, Himself will ope Heaven's gate,

And His sweet Bride proclaim the pardon vast.

THE DOVE.

" In the inmost being of every man is a sanctuary of everlasting
being; wherein, in man's true craving for salvation, the everlasting
Godhead enters to make it His dwelling place."

BIBLICAL PSYCHOLOGY. DELITZSCH.

Weary with flying o'er the watery waste,

    Finding no tree nor any place of rest,

To my belovèd one I flew in haste,

    And folded my wild wings upon his breast,—

" Oh! art thou come at last, my hidden part?"

He cried, " Thou soul of my eternal heart!"

THE NEW COVENANT.

" Behold, the days come, saith the Lord, that I will make a new covenant with the house of Israel, and with the house of Judah :

" This shall be the covenant that I will make with the house of Israel ; After those days, saith the Lord, I will put my law in their inward parts, and write it in their hearts; and will be their God, and they shall be my people."—JEREMIAH xxxi. 31, 33.

" Morever I will make a covenant of peace with them : it shall be an everlasting covenant with them : and I will place them, and multiply them, and will set my sanctuary in the midst of them for evermore.

" My tabernacle also shall be with them ; yea, I will be their God, and they shall be my people.

" And the heathen shall know that I the Lord do sanctify Israel, when my sanctuary shall be in the midst of them for evermore."

EZEKIEL xxxvii. 26-28.

"I will dwell in them, and walk in them ; and I will be their God, and they shall be my people.

" And I will receive you, and will be a Father unto you, and ye shall be my sons and daughters, saith the Lord Almighty."

II. CORINTHIANS vi. 16-18.

" And the Word was made flesh, and dwelt among us, (and we beheld his glory, the glory as of the only begotten of the Father,) full of grace and truth."—JOHN i. 14.

" In his days Judah shall be saved, and Israel shall dwell safely ; and this is his name whereby he shall be called, 'The Lord our Righteousness.'"—JEREMIAH xxiii. 6.

" Eye hath not seen nor ear heard, neither have entered into the heart of man, the things which God hath prepared for them that love him. But God hath revealed them unto us by his Spirit."

I. CORINTHIANS ii. 9, 10

The air is filled with thoughts of thee,

  I dream of thee, asleep, awake ;

  My heart doth golden silence break

With silver chords of minstrelsy ;

In songs of summer melody

  My voice is lifted for thy sake.

My harp I laid aside with tears,—

  Again is tuned to silver sound,

  Its strings beneath thy touch rebound

With echoes of my youthful years,

And many a lost hope re-appears

  Like blossoms springing from the ground.

The violet's dewy eye is there,

   The wind-flower lifts its sweet shy face,

   Hepaticas, with modest grace,

Shed their faint odours on the air ;

The spring is sweet, the earth is fair,

   Because it is thy dwelling place.

The spring is sweet because of thee ;

   And soon the rose will blush more red,

   Because that love, once counted dead,

Has risen to brighter victory ;

And over land and over sea

   The rosy light of love hath spread,—

The rosy light of love's new morn ;

   Because of thee the earth is glad,

   Because of thee the earth is clad

In brighter green ; the spring, re-born.

Bids nature now, no more forlorn,

Forget her woes and sorrows sad.

Because of thee, thou loveliest one,

Each starry flower more brightly glows,

A sweeter fragrance fills the rose,

The moss is greener on the stone,—

I cannot love thee, love, alone,

Thy sweetness through all nature flows.

And all earth's nascent life is thrilled

With love outpoured from me to thee ;

The ripples of the flowing sea,

With a diviner music filled,

Bid warnings cease—discords are stilled—

From heaven descends new harmony.

Yea, heavenly airs about us blow,

   And heavenly music breathes its voice,

   And bids our human hearts rejoice ;

With rapture all shall learn to know

When heaven and earth together flow

   In mutual love and mutual choice.

Beneath there is not any deep,

   Nor any highest height above,—

   Man cannot pierce with wings of love ;

Nor any way of love too steep

For those who God's commandments keep,

   And His eternal mandates prove.

THE PERFECT LAW.

God gives us songs to lighten weary days,

And dreams celestial—visions of the night ;

Through day, a cloud,—in darkness, fiery bright,—

His pillar leads us on through devious ways,

Bids us advance, and then our steps it stays ;

In peaceful rest, in swift victorious fight,

His arm doth shelter us, and His great might

Endues with strength while one a hundred slays.

Thou art the living God, and Thee we serve,

We have no other God, O Lord, but Thee !

Thy law engraven, now, on every nerve,

In every inward part Thy Word we see,

And from Thy perfect law we cannot swerve,

Since hearts do hold the truth that makes them free.

THE LOVE OF CHRIST.

" Thou shalt call his name Jesus, for he shall save his people from their sins."—MATTHEW i. 21.

" That Christ may dwell in your hearts by faith ; that ye, being rooted and grounded in love, may be able to comprehend with all saints what is the breadth, and length, and depth, and height ;

"And to know the love of Christ, which passeth knowledge, that ye might be filled with all the fulness of God."

EPHESIANS iii. 17-19.

"And walk in love, as Christ also hath loved us, and hath given himself for us an offering and a sacrifice to God for a sweet-smelling savour."—EPHESIANS v. 2.

" For I am persuaded, that neither death, nor life, nor angels, nor principalities, nor powers, nor things present, nor things to come,

" Nor height, nor depth, nor any other creature, shall be able to separate us from the love of God, which is in Christ Jesus our Lord."—ROMANS viii. 38, 39.

Higher, and higher burns the flame,

The sacrificial fire ;

Deeper, and deeper glows the Name

To which our hearts aspire ;

The Son, ascending whence he came,

Descends at love's desire ;

His mercy round about us flows,
  His love our being thrills ;
Blushes a deeper red the rose ;
  Diviner music fills
The southern air that round us blows
  From far-off sacred hills.

Sweet is the smell of tender vines,
  And sweet the budding spring ;
In vineyards, down the steep inclines,
  The blossoms, clustering,
Are spreading far their fragrant signs
  Of fruitful gathering.

O sunny land where lilies bloom !
  And where the wild flowers spread,
Weaving a carpet, like a loom—
  Sad blue and golden red,
Fit purples for a royal tomb
  Emblazoned for the dead.

O land where our great fathers sleep,—

    The mighty men of old,

Who watched their flocks and called their sheep

    By name into each fold ;

Shall not lost Israel's Shepherd keep

    The names by Love foretold ?

Elected now by special grace,

    Called forth by deed and sign,

The remnant of the chosen race—

    To hold the power divine,

And bring each prophet to his place

    Beneath his tree and vine.

Again the mighty hand puts forth ;

    The Thunderer's oath is heard ;

By mingled tones of love and wrath

The slumbering bones are stirred ;
From east to west, from south to north,
The power of life conferred.

Awake ! lost Israel, awake !
  Behold your rising sun,
Your golden day begins to break,
  Your sabbath hath begun.
The nations, blessed for thy sake,
  Toward thy Light shall run.

An ensign for the nations, set
  As stones within a crown,
Proclaiming God cannot forget,
  Nor love by floods be drown ;
Behold His people living yet,
  A nation of renown.

Behold His righteous oath fulfilled
  In Abraham's chosen seed,—
The holy land again is tilled
  By husbandmen indeed ;
His word is fruitful as He willed,
  Replenished every need.

Yea, we shall live in Abraham's land,
  Beneath the holy sky,—
A little flock, a chosen band,
  The apple of God's eye,
Gathered again by His right hand,—
  A blessèd company.

He is the Rock, His way is plain,
  And we His portion are ;
Though we by our own sins were slain,

Those sins are set afar,

And love hath planted us again,

  And healed each wound and scar.

Redeemed we are by love's great might

  The Lord, our Righteousness,

Hath set us up in all men's sight,

  That we might all men bless ;

Our robes in blood were washèd white—

  That blood we now confess.

Jesus, the Christ, Immanuel,

  Hath washed away our stains,

And He within our hearts doth dwell,

  His throne in us regains ;

Let heavenly choirs our rapture tell,

  In high seraphic strains.

Yea, let the choirs in heaven above,

And tribes on earth below,

Sing praises to the King of love,

Whose mercies round us flow,

Who gave His life that He might prove

That love all souls must know.

VALEDICTION.

VALEDICTION.

To Israel's scattered house, my songs I send.—
May mighty tones with my meek accents blend :
May cloven tongues of bright celestial fire,
Proclaim the coming of each heart's desire.
That Israel, dwelling in all lands, may hear,
In its own speech, prophetic voices clear
Declaring mercy deep, and broad, and vast.
Exiled, and hidden, sinner, and outcast.
May each, in Christ, their God Incarnate see,
And know that Jesus fills humanity
With Father's boundless love—a flowing tide,
That knowledge of the Lord sweeps far and wide ;
As seas about the broad earth sweep and roam,
So love of God doth seek to call men home,—
His chosen ones unto their land of rest,
His children all to Paradise most blest.

For Israel cast away the Gentiles brought,

And Israel now, with love, by Gentiles sought,

Shall be as precious gems within His crown,

Shall build the house of bread—King David's town.

O Israel, to holiness restored,

Call all mankind to love and praise the Lord;

Let fountains gush, and clear pure rivers flow,

'Till every soul shall learn its God to know ;

Raise Abraham and Sarah from their tomb,

And let their land with sweetest blossoms bloom ;

Let Israel camp upon her ancient hills,

And know that God His sacred oath fulfils.

The righteous Shepherd-King to us descends

To feed his precious flock—His lambs he tends

With gentle care, He leadeth them beside

The waters still, and in His breast doth hide

The feeble ones, the lost He doth reclaim,

And calleth each one tenderly by name ;

So gentle is His look, so meek His speech,

It doth the hardest melt, the stoniest reach ;

All willing hearts may know him as their Friend.

May feel His loving hands above them bend,

May all the joys of His sweet comfort taste,—

For at His feet flowers spring in desert waste,

And gushing waters in dry sands abound,

And shadowing Rock in sultry land is found ;

New earth, new deeps beneath, new heavens above,

Proclaim, in rapturous tones, that God is Love ;

Mankind, the tidings glad at last believing,

The boundless, endless, love of God receiving,

Becomes the Temple-throne where King may dwell,

Brings forth, with joy, the Child Immanuel.

" O most gracious and deep love of God in Christ Jesus, I beseech thee grant me thy Pearl, impress it into my Soul, and take my Soul into Thine arms."

JACOB BEHMEN.

CONTENTS.

CONTENTS.

Part III.

THE CASTLE OF THE SOUL.

Part IV.

THE NEW EARTH.

CONTENTS

Fscp. 8vo., Cloth.

THE TRIUMPH OF LOVE.

A

Mystical Poem

IN SONGS, SONNETS, AND VERSE.

BY

ELLA DIETZ.

LONDON:
E. W. ALLEN, 4, AVE MARIA LANE,
AND STATIONERS' HALL COURT.
MDCCCLXXVII.

THE ENGLISH PRESS.

THE EXAMINER.

There is no ordinary depth and tenderness of feeling in these
poems. They have a curious resemblance in sentiment to the
mystical poetry of the seventeenth century. Such a song as the
following might have been written by a female George Herbert :—

> "O touch me not, unless thy soul
>   Can claim my soul as thine;
> Give me no earthly flowers that fade,
>   No love, but love divine :
> For I gave thee immortal flowers,
> That bloomed serene in heavenly bowers.
>
> Look not with favour on my face,
>   Nor answer my caress,
> Unless my soul have first found grace
>   Within thy sight; express
> Only the truth, though it should be
> Cold as the ice on northern sea.
>
> O never speak of love to me,
>   Unless thy heart can feel
> That in the face of Deity
>   Thou wouldst that love reveal :
> For God is love, and His bright law
> Should find our hearts without one flaw."

THE ACADEMY.

If the book is simply an expression of human love, it is very
graceful and full of poetical feeling. In their first and obvious
meaning some of the sonnets are beautiful. We quote one from
the early part of the book :—

> "Should we part now? O love, how can we part?
> Leave if thou wilt, thou canst not take away
> The glory and the brightness of the day.
> My soul will be with thine where'er thou art :
> Till thou canst send the red blood from thy heart
> Thou canst not banish me, though I may stay
> As silently; still shall my silence pray
> Until thy spirit feel the vital smart.

A A 2

> I would not have thee suffer. O my own,
> I would not hold thee, thou shouldst still be free,
> For when thou goest I am not alone,
> Thou canst not take thyself away from me : ᵕ
> But thou canst dim the brightness of the sun
> With clouds. O love! I would not have thee gone !"

SUNDAY TIMES.

Few volumes of modern poetry deserve a warmer welcome than *The Triumph of Love* of Miss Ella Dietz. Tender, thoughtful, and womanly throughout, it rises at points into absolute inspiration, and it has every variety of charm that cultivation, fervent aspiration, and poetic perception can bestow. Its attractions for the reader will be increased when he knows that the author is an artist who has won herself position upon the stage. A work must, of course, stand upon its own merits and be judged apart from all personal claim of the author. When, however, tested by the most rigid standard, it wins admiration, the fact that the author has claims of another class cannot fail to enhance the interest it possesses.

Not so accustomed, indeed, are our artists to go out of themselves and seek distinction in kindred walks that we can be otherwise than grateful when we find an instance such as this in question.

We accord thus a warm reception to a book that needs no such recommendation, for the fact that its writer is one who has won our admiration by the display of other phases of her talent.

As Miss Dietz supplies as the second title of her book the words " A Mystical Poem," it is pardonable on our part if we fail to grasp its entire significance or to set before our readers the full scope of its aim. Not at all the kind of victory ordinarily chaunted is the triumph Miss Dietz sings. To those who look only on the surface of things that may, indeed, seem like defeat which is advanced as victory. The crown of martyrdom, phantom-like as is its circlet, is, in fact, as real as those " golden rounds " which have come to stand as the symbol of authority. Love stronger than death, love immortal, living beyond the grave, love that

> " Lives and spreads aloft by those pure eyes,
> And perfect witness of all-judging Jove."

is what she sings. A sonnet from the Portuguese of Mrs. Barrett Browning, who is evidently a strong favourite of the modern poetess, might, indeed, serve as a motto to the volume. The sonnet referred to is that familiar one commencing

> "How do I love thee, let me count thy ways,"

and ending

> " If God please,
> I shall but love thee better after death."

Two lines, indeed, from the author's own prologue, might serve the same purpose. They are as follows:

> "And fight once fought, the crown's forever won,
> For what God doeth cannot be undone."

It is involved in the very conditions under which a poem like this is written that it is impossible to give by separate extracts an idea of the sustained grace, beauty and tenderness of the whole. This, however, is the only resource left us. The reader who seeks to comprehend the relation to each other of the different portions headed by such names as " Retrospection," "Introspection," " The Reality," " The Temptation," and " The Triumph," the re-current sweetness of the refrains or the pathos of the " Interludes " must turn to the volume.

THE PHYSCHOLOGICAL REVIEW.

Every true poet, yea, every original thinker, is a mystical teacher for some stage of initiation into the hidden life, and every one by birthright has entered into one or more of its degrees. He is more immediately and widely heard who can give expression to the mystic feeling of the greater number. * * * The writer seems to have drank deeply of the well of our best Elizabethan poets ; some verses remind us of Spenser, and the unity of purpose and subject of the sonnets of those of Shakespere.

The poem called " Emanation " reads like pages of Jacob Böhme turned into musical verse, and gaining in force and clearness by the translation ; it is suggestive of the true origin and progress of species.

THE TRIUMPH OF TIME.

Mystical Poem.

BY

ELLA DIETZ.

A SEQUEL TO "THE TRIUMPH OF LOVE."

——————

LONDON:

E. W. ALLEN. 4, AVE MARIA LANE.

MDCCCLXXXIV.

——

THE ENGLISH PRESS.

THE ACADEMY.

The Triumph of Time. By Ella Dietz. (E. W. Allen.) Miss Dietz's name was familiar in London two or three years ago as that of a young actress and public reader. Since then, the lady has spent some time in America in the pursuit of her profession, and the English public have heard but little of her. Shortly before leaving England, she published a mystical poem entitled *The Triumph of Love*, and it is as a sequel to that work that the present book is published. Like its predecessor, the new poem is chiefly remarkable for a somewhat vivid delineation of ascetic passion. It has a pathetic and obvious human interest, quite apart from its hidden intention. Indeed, we must frankly confess to some unwillingness to dig beneath the surface for the meaning of Miss Dietz's work. The psychical problems that lie buried beneath a series of short poems, which tell the simple story of the triumph of time over love, need not be disturbed in their tomb. Setting aside the mystical pretensions of Miss Dietz's book, we find much to commend in its sweetness and simplicity, its directness and force. There is the ease of mastery in not a few of these poems. The writer knows what she can do, and does it without effort. Certain of the slighter pieces show that Miss Dietz has studied Goethe's lyrics and ballads to some purpose.

> " Let those who will forget
>   Love's sacred ways ;
> Mine eyes with tears are wet
>   For love's lost days.
>
> Mine eyes with tears are wet
>   My heart is sad,
> Let those who will forget
>   To make it glad."

There is a pure and tender womanliness in everything this book contains. There are a few ambitious poems in the volume—poems in which the simple human significance of a situation does not

serve, and symbol is aimed after. Of these, the best is the sonnet
headed, "Waters in the Desert." It does no injustice to Miss
Christina Rossetti to say that, but for the cumbrousness of the
tenth line, the following might almost be mistaken for her writing :—

> " Long time I wandered in a barren land,
>   My stumbling feet beset by unknown ways,
>   The scorching sun blinding my weary gaze,
> A brazen sky above a waste of sand,
>   No shelter from the torturing burning rays:
>   O God! I cried, end now my nights and days,
> Smite me with death, yea, strike me where I stand.
> And Thou didst smite, as Moses smote the rock,
>   Not unto death, for forth there gushing flowed
>   A stream of life, and suddenly there glowed
> Bright roses where had been an earthquake's shock.
>   And grasses green appeared, and cattle lowed,
> And by a stream a shepherd fed his flock."

THE LITERARY WORLD.

The Triumph of Time. A mystical poem of considerable power
and beauty, composed of lyrics and sonnets on the varying
phases of religious feeling and human love. A rare grace and
a tender beauty breathe in these strange songs. The flow of
the verse is as easy as if the writer's thought was metrical.
One is surprised to find so little demand made on the tolerance
for obscurity which is generally accorded to mystical poetry.
Some of these sonnets are of uncommon excellence—for example,
the series entitled " When Beauty Fades," from which we give
the second :—

> So I be fair to thee, I care not when
>   I loose the bloom that other eyes admire;
>   When I lose grace for thee let kind hands 'tire
> Me in my burial-robes and hide me; then
> I shall have lived too long in sight of men
>   If thy love fickle prove; let me retire
>   To some dim solitude, and there expire
> Alone, forgotten. out of sight and ken.
> Tell me what grace in me first won thy heart?
>   What didst thou find in me worthy to prize?
> Oh! was it not for some immortal part
>   Rather than for that fair which fades and dies?
> Didst thou not say, " I love thee as thou art
>   And as thou shalt be when the dead shall rise?"

" The Wingèd Harp " and " Henceforth I will believe that thou
dost love " are equally well worth quoting. It is peculiarly difficult
to make selections from this poem, because in many instances a
great part of the happy effect of sonnet or song is due to its
position, and is dependent on what precedes and follows. Just as
in a beautiful country the artist finds it impossible to satisfy
himself with a prospect that will fit into the limits of a picture, and
as no musician will offer a few bars as a specimen of a sonata, so
from this poem of sudden transition of thought, and feeling, and
metre, we cannot cull without injustice. Yet, notwithstanding our
scruples about cutting and carving, we must have a few verses
from the " Hymn of Praise."

> Father of all, who hast given the dawn and the dew,
>   The night and the stars, which are but as shadows of Thee ;
> We bathe in Thy light, and our souls are reborn and made new,
>   We kneel in Thy sight, and arise with our pinions set free.
>
> Thou hast given us songs for our joy, and laments for our sorrow,
>   Thou hast given the rushing of rivers, the murmurs of seas,
> Thou hast given us dreams of the night, and new life on the morrow,
>   Thy hand is the hand that hath made and hath given us these.
>
>   *   *   *   *   *
>
> Each June brings its roses, the shadows of roses supernal,
>   Each autumn its vintage, its harvest of fruits and of flowers,
> And these blessings of earth are but types of the blessings eternal,
>   Eternal as time with its pageant of days and of hours.
>
> Oh ! hide not Thy face nor Thy light, though in darkness thou shinest,
>   We know and acknowledge that Thou art our Lord and our God ;
> Without Thee all pleasures are dead, and joys e'en the divinest
>   Become as the dust of the earth which our feet have downtrod.

THE CHURCH REFORMER.

REVIEW. *The Triumph of Time.* Mystical Poem. By Ella Dietz.
A Mystical Poem runs the risk of obtaining but few readers in
these days in which men boast, with what terribly ludicrous
results, of being so practical. We hope in some future numbers
to be able to offer to our readers a few papers on Mysticism
by the anthoress of this volume. Of this poem we would say
that any one who is in the habit of making a reverential study

of the Holy Scriptures both of the Old and New Testament, will find it in much to help them and a good deal to suggest new thoughts. That the writer is one of the most exquisite "Rosalinds" ever seen on the stage will perhaps induce some to read the book who would otherwise have been frightened by its description as "mystical": and will also perhaps make them demand much more than they get in the ordinary interpreters of "Rosalind." We quote a few verses from "The Virgin Mother":—

"They have no wine" the Mother said
To Him who was the fountain head
　Of wine the great joy giver;
"They have no wine;" the vessels fill
With water, and the Royal will
　Made wine flow like a river.

"They have no wine," the Mother prays
E'en now when tearful voices raise
　Their tones of sad repenting
O blessed Mother-prayers, prevail
To bring forth wine that shall prevail
　To heal past all relenting.

O Thou who art the very vine
From which flows forth the living wine
　Strengthen our feeble praying;
Sweet Mother Mary near us stand.
The people faint make swift demand,
　Our need brooks no delaying.

　＊　　　　＊　　　　＊　　　　＊

Mother all joy is withered
From men let tender words be said,
　To call down marriage blessing,
Speak to thy Son but once again,
Bring joy unto the sons of men,
　Yea, rapture past expressing.

Thou blessed Virgin Mother mild
Who nurturdest at thy breast the child
　For which the earth is groaning;
Breathe words of wisdom in our ear
That hungering, thirsting hearts may hear
　And cease their restless moaning

Fresh springs of joy are found in Thee
Tabors and pipes and minstrelsy,
　And ecstacy of motion;

Who made the birds' swift-winged grace,
The courser—fleet to run his race,
  The finny tribes of ocean.

From thee all human joy doth spring,
The insect world on gauzy wing
  Quivers with exultation—
And shall not man as happy find
His wealth of joy in one great Mind
  That formed the whole creation.

There is no joy but what He gives,
Supremest joy within Him lives,
  Yea, joy beyond comparing;
Reject Him and we suffer loss,
Nailing His love upon the cross;
  Such grief must God be sharing.